Selected Adventures of

Sherlock Holmes

by

Sir Arthur Conan Doyle

CORE CLASSICS®

SERIES EDITOR MICHAEL J. MARSHALL

ABRIDGET BY NORMAN J. WOOLWPRTH

LIBRARY OF CONGRESS CATALOG CARD NUMBER: 97-077397

ISBN 978-1-890517-08-3 TRADE PAPERBACK

PRINTED IN CANADA

COVER ILLUSTRATION BY GB mMcINTOSH

TEXT ILLUSTRATIONS BY SIDNEY PAGET 1891-92

CORE KNOWLEDGE FOUNDATION

801 EAST HIGH STREET

CHARLOTTESVILLE, VIRGINIA 22902

www.coreknowledge.org

Contents

Introduction

At the time Sir Arthur Conan Doyle created Sherlock Holmes, the most famous detective in fiction, most stories were told in parts in magazines over many months. The problem with that, Doyle thought, was that if readers happened to miss the first part, they would not be interested in picking up the story later. So he decided to write stories that were complete in one issue and had main characters that reappeared in future adventures. Edgar Allan Poe wrote the first detective story, but Doyle reinvented it with the characters of Sherlock Holmes and Dr. John Watson.

One reason people like to read detective stories is because in real life crimes can go unsolved and unpunished. A crime causes disorder. A detective's job is to solve the crime so our social relationships can be put back in order. The heroes of detective stories show how even very puzzling crimes can be explained. This helps us believe that justice is still possible.

Sometimes Holmes solves mysteries that do not involve a crime. But in any case, his techniques are the same. First, he makes keen observations. He looks very closely at what the details of a person's appearance reveal. Second, he is strictly logical. He always finds as many facts about a case as he can before he starts thinking about a theory that would fit them together. Third, he is ready to use disguises and a little trickery to find clues. Furthermore, Holmes always tries to learn more general knowledge so that he can have a greater chance of solving new problems. He also studies the history of crime so that he can compare his cases with other instances of mysterious and wicked behavior.

Just as vivid to us as Holmes, with his deerstalker cap, his caped overcoat, his pipe and his handy magnifying glass, is his companion Dr. Watson, who narrates these adventures. A war veteran and a married man, Dr. Watson adds common sense and coolness in the face of danger to Holmes's brilliant reasoning.

Doyle's storytelling made this pair seem so real that his fans tend to speak of the sleuth and his sidekick as if they were actual historical people and not simply made-up figures. In Doyle's day, Sherlock Holmes became so hugely popular that Doyle decided he must write a story in which Holmes died in order to be free to write about a different subject. So he suggested that Holmes plunged to his death in a gorge while wrestling the evil genius Professor Moriarty. Readers howled in protest. Even Doyle's mother told him he was wrong. Doyle gave in and began writing more Holmes stories.

E. D. Hirsch Jr.

Charlottesville, Virginia

Sherlock Holmes

The Speckled Band

Of the many cases in which I have studied the methods of Sherlock Holmes, I cannot recall any more remarkable than that associated with the well-known family of the Roylotts of Stoke Moran. These events occurred in the early days of my association with Holmes, when we were sharing rooms as bachelors, in Baker Street.

I woke one morning to find Sherlock Holmes standing, fully dressed, by the side of my bed. He was a late riser as a rule, and, as the clock on the mantelpiece showed me that it was only a quarter past seven, I blinked up at him in some surprise.

"Sorry to wake you up, Watson," said he. "Mrs. Hudson has been woken up, she woke me, and I you."

"What is it, then? A fire?"

"No, a client. It seems that a young lady has arrived in a state of excitement who insists upon seeing me. She is waiting now in the sitting room. Now, when young ladies wander about the city at this hour of the morning and rouse sleepy people up out of their beds, I presume they have something very pressing to communicate. Should it be an interesting case, you would, I am sure, wish to follow it from the outset. I thought at any rate that I should give you the chance."

"My dear fellow, I would not miss it for anything."

I had no keener pleasure than in following Holmes in his investigations. I admired the rapid deductions, always founded on a logical basis, with which he unravelled problems. I rapidly threw on my clothes and was ready in a few minutes to accompany my friend down to the sitting room. A lady, dressed in black and heavily veiled, rose as we entered.

"Good morning, madam," said Holmes.

"My name is Sherlock Holmes. This is my close friend, Dr. Watson, before whom you can speak freely. Ha, I am glad to see that Mrs. Hudson has had the good sense to light the fire. Pray draw up to it, and I shall

SHE RAISED HER VEIL AS SHE SPOKE.

order you a cup of hot coffee, for I observe that you are shivering."

"It is not cold that makes me shiver," said the woman, changing her seat as requested.

"What, then?"

"It is fear, Mr. Holmes. It is terror." She raised her veil as she spoke, and we could see that she was indeed in a state of agitation, her face all drawn and grey.

Her features and figure were those of a woman of thirty, but her hair was grey, and her expression was weary.

"You must not fear," said Holmes soothingly. "We shall soon set matters right, I have no doubt. You have come in by train this morning, I see."

"You know me, then?"

"No, but I observe half of a return ticket in your glove. You must have started early, and yet you had a good drive in a dogcart, along heavy roads, before you reached the station."

The lady stared in bewilderment at my companion.

"There is no mystery, my dear madam," said he, smiling. "The left arm of your jacket is spattered with mud in seven places. The marks are perfectly fresh. No vehicle except a dogcart throws up mud in that way, and then only when you sit on the left side of the driver."

"Whatever your reasons may be, you are perfectly correct," said she. "Sir, I can stand this strain no longer; I shall go mad if it continues. I have no one to turn to. I have heard of you, Mr. Holmes. Oh, sir, do you think you could help me? At present it is out of my power to reward you for your services, but in a month or two I shall be married, with my own income, and then you shall not find me ungrateful."

"I can only say, madam, that I shall be happy to take on your case. As to reward, my profession is its reward. And now I beg that you will lay before us everything that may help us in forming an opinion upon the matter."

"Alas!" replied our visitor. "The horror of my situation lies in the fact that my fears are so vague, and my suspicions depend upon small points, which might seem trivial to another. But I have heard, Mr. Holmes, that you can see deeply into the wickedness of the human heart. Advise me how to walk amid the dangers that encompass me."

"I am all attention, madam."

"My name is Helen Stoner. I live with my stepfather, who is the last survivor of one of the oldest Saxon families in England, the Roylotts of Stoke Moran, on the western border of Surrey."

"The name is familiar to me," said he.

"The family was once among the richest in England. In the last century, however, four successive heirs were of a wasteful nature, and the family ruin was completed by a gambler. Nothing was left except a few acres and the two-hundred-year-old house. The last squire dragged out his existence there, living the life of an aristocratic **pauper**. But his only son, my stepfather, seeing that he must adapt to new conditions, obtained a medical degree and went to India, where he established a large practice. In a fit of anger, however, he beat his native butler to death and narrowly escaped a death sentence. As it was, he suffered a long imprisonment and later returned to England a disappointed man.

PAUPER
Someone who is very poor.

"When Dr. Roylott was in India he married my mother, Mrs. Stoner, the young widow of Major-General Stoner, of the Bengal Artillery. My sister Julia and I were twins, and we were only two years old at the time of my mother's re-marriage. She had a considerable sum of money, and this she left to Dr. Roylott entirely while we resided with him, with a provision that a certain annual sum should be given to each of us in the event of our marriage. Shortly after our return to England my mother died in a railway accident. Dr. Roylott then took us to live with him in the ancestral house at Stoke Moran. The money which my mother had left was enough for all our wants, and there seemed no obstacle to our happiness.

"But a terrible change came over our stepfather about this time. Instead of making friends and exchanging visits with our neighbors, who had at first been overjoyed to see a Roylott back in the old family seat, he shut himself up in his house. He seldom came out except to quarrel ferociously with whoever might cross his path. Violence of temper has been hereditary in the men of the family, and in my stepfather's case it had, I believe, been intensified by his long residence in the tropics. A series of disgraceful brawls took place, two of which ended in the police court. He became the terror of the village. Folks would fly at his approach, for he is a man of immense strength and absolutely uncontrollable anger.

"Last week he hurled the local blacksmith off a bridge into a stream, and it was only by paying all the money that I could gather that I was able to avert another public disclosure. He had no friends at all except the wandering gypsies, and he would allow them to camp on the few acres of bramble-covered land that represent the family estate. He would wander away with them sometimes for weeks on end. He has a passion also for Indian animals, and he has at this moment a cheetah and a baboon. They wander freely over his grounds and are

HE HURLED THE BLACKSMITH OFF A BRIDGE.

feared by the villagers almost as much as their master.

"You can imagine from what I say that my poor sister Julia and I had no great pleasure in our lives. No servant would stay with us, and for a long time we did all the work of the house. She was only thirty at the time of her death, yet her hair had begun to whiten, just as mine has."

"Your sister is dead, then?"

"She died just two years ago, and it is of her death that I wish to speak to you. You can understand that, living as I have described, we were not likely to see anyone of our own age. We had, however, an aunt, who lives near Harrow, and we were occasionally allowed to pay short visits at her house. Julia went there at Christmas two years ago and met a Major of Marines, to whom she became engaged. My stepfather offered no objection to the marriage. But within two weeks of the wedding day, the terrible event occurred that has deprived me of my only companion."

Sherlock Holmes had been leaning back in his chair with his eyes closed, and his head sunk in a cushion, but he half opened his lids now and glanced across at his visitor.

"Pray be precise as to the details," said he.

"It is easy for me to be so, for every event of that dreadful time is seared into my memory. The manor house is, as I have already said, very old, and only one wing is now inhabited. The bedrooms in this wing are on the ground floor. Of these bedrooms, the first is Dr. Roylott's, the second my sister's, and the third my own. There are no doors between them, but they all open out into the same corridor. Do I make myself plain?"

"Perfectly so."

"The windows of the three rooms open out upon the lawn. That fatal night Dr. Roylott had gone to his room early, though we knew he had not gone to sleep, for my sister was troubled by the smell of the strong Indian cigars that it was his custom to smoke. She left her room, and came into mine, where we chatted about her wedding. At eleven o'clock she rose to leave me, but she paused at the door and looked back.

" 'Tell me, Helen,' said she, 'have you ever heard anyone whistle in the dead of the night?'

" 'Never,' said I.

" 'I suppose that you could not possibly whistle yourself in your sleep?'

" 'Certainly not. But why?'

" 'Because during the last few nights I have, about three in the morning, heard a low clear whistle. I am a light sleeper, and it has awakened me. I cannot tell where it came from – perhaps from the next room, perhaps from the lawn. I thought that I would just ask you whether you had heard it.'

" 'No. It must be those wretched gypsies.'

" 'Very likely. And yet if it were on the lawn, I wonder why you did not hear it also.'

" 'I sleep more heavily than you.'

" 'Well, it is of no consequence, at any rate.' She smiled at me, closed my door, and a few moments later I heard her key turn in the lock."

"Indeed," said Holmes. "Was it your custom always to lock yourselves in at night?"

"Always."

"And why?"

"I think I mentioned that the Doctor kept a cheetah and a baboon. We had no feeling of security unless our doors were locked."

"Quite so. Pray proceed."

"I could not sleep that night. A vague feeling of

misfortune troubled me. It was a wild night. The wind was howling outside, and the rain was beating and splashing against the windows. Suddenly, there burst forth the scream of a terrified woman. I knew that it was my sister's voice. I sprang from my bed and rushed into the corridor. As I opened my door I seemed to hear a low whistle, such as my sister described, and a few moments later a clanging sound, as if a metal object had fallen. As I ran down the passage, my sister's door was open. I stared at it horror-stricken, not knowing what was about to emerge from it. By the light of the corridor lamp I saw my sister appear at the opening, her face blanched with terror, her hands groping for help, her whole figure swaying to and fro like that of a drunkard. I ran to her and threw my arms around her. At that moment her knees seemed to give way and she fell to the ground. She writhed in terrible pain, and her limbs were dreadfully convulsed. At first I thought she had not recognized me, but as I bent over her she suddenly shrieked out in a voice I shall never forget, 'O, my God! Helen! It was the band! The speckled band!' She stabbed with her finger into the air in the direction of the Doctor's room, but a convulsion seized her and choked her words. I rushed

I SAW MY SISTER APPEAR, HER FACE BLANCHED WITH TERROR.

out, calling loudly for my stepfather, and I met him hastening from his room in his dressing-gown. When he reached my sister's side she was unconscious, and though he sent for medical aid from the village, all efforts were in vain, for she slowly sank and died without having recovered her consciousness. Such was the dreadful end of my beloved sister."

"One moment," said Holmes. "Are you sure about this whistle and metallic sound?"

"That was what the **coroner** asked me at the inquiry. It is my strong impression that I heard it, and yet among the crash of the gale, I may possibly have been deceived."

CORONER
A public official who investigates deaths.

"Was your sister dressed?"

"No, she was in her nightdress. In her hand was the charred stump of a match."

"Showing that she had struck a light and looked about her. That is important. And what conclusions did the coroner come to?"

"He investigated the case with great care, for Dr. Roylott's conduct had long been notorious, but he was unable to find any cause of death. My evidence showed that the door had been fastened on the inside, and the windows were blocked by old-fashioned shutters with iron bars, which were secured every night. The walls were shown to be quite solid all around, and the flooring was also thoroughly examined, with the same result. It is certain, therefore, that my sister was alone when she met her end. Besides, there were no marks of any violence upon her."

"How about poison?"

"The doctors examined her for it, but without success."

"What do you think that this unfortunate lady died of, then?"

"It is my belief that she died of pure fear and nervous shock, though what it was that frightened her I cannot imagine."

"Were there gypsies on the estate?"

"Yes, there are nearly always some there."

"Ah, and what did you gather from this reference to a band – a speckled band?"

"Sometimes I have thought that it was merely the wild talk of delirium, sometimes that it may have referred to the gypsies. I do not know whether the spotted handkerchiefs that many of them wear on their heads might have suggested the strange adjective that she used."

Holmes shook his head like a man who is far from being satisfied. "These are very deep waters," said he. "Pray go on with your story."

"Two years have passed since then, and my life has been lonelier than ever. A month ago, however, a dear friend asked my hand in marriage. My stepfather offered no opposition, and we are to be married in the spring. Two days ago some repairs were started in the west wing of the building, so that I have had to move into the room in which my sister died, and to sleep in the very bed in which she slept. Imagine, then, my terror when last night, as I lay awake, I suddenly heard in the silence of the night the low whistle that heralded her own death. I sprang up and lit the lamp, but nothing was to be seen in the room. I was too shaken to go to bed again, however, so I dressed, and as soon as it was daylight I got a dogcart at the Crown Inn and drove to Leatherhead, from whence I have come this morning to ask your advice."

"You have done wisely," said my friend. "But have you told me all?"

"Yes, all."

There was a long silence, during which Holmes leaned his chin upon his hands.

"This is very deep business," he said at last. "There are a thousand details that I should desire to know before I decide upon our course of action. Yet we have not a moment to lose. If we were to come to Stoke

Moran today, would it be possible for us to see these rooms without the knowledge of your stepfather?"

"As it happens, he came to town today on some important business. It is probable that he will be away all day, and that there would be nothing to disturb you."

"Excellent. You are not averse to this trip, Watson?"

"By no means."

"Then we shall both come. What are you going to do, Miss Stoner?"

"I have one or two things that I would wish to do now that I am in town. But I shall return by the twelve o'clock train, so as to be there in time for your coming."

"And you may expect us early in the afternoon. I have myself some small business matters to attend to. Will you not breakfast?"

"No, I must go. My heart is lightened since I have confided my trouble to you. I look forward to seeing you again this afternoon." She dropped her black veil over her face and glided from the room.

"And what do you think of it all, Watson?" asked Holmes, leaning back in his chair.

"It seems to me a most sinister business."

"Dark enough and sinister enough."

"Yet if the lady is correct in saying that the flooring and walls are sound, and that the door, window, and chimney are impassable, then her sister must have been alone when she met her mysterious end."

"What, then, of these whistles in the night and the peculiar words of the dying woman?"

"I cannot think."

"When you combine the ideas of whistles at night, the presence of a band of gypsies who are on intimate terms with this old doctor, the fact that we have reason to believe that the doctor has an interest in preventing his stepdaughter's marriage, the dying reference to a band, and finally, the fact that Miss Helen Stoner heard a metallic clang, which might have been caused by one of those metal bars that secured the shutters falling back into place, I think that the mystery may be cleared along those lines."

"But what, then, did the gypsies do?"

"I cannot imagine."

"I see many objections to any such a theory."

"And so do I. It is precisely for that reason that we are going to Stoke Moran this day. But what, in the

A HUGE MAN ENTERED, WHOSE DEEP EYES AND THIN NOSE GAVE HIM THE LOOK OF A FIERCE OLD BIRD OF PREY.

name of the devil!"

Our door had suddenly flung open, and a huge man entered. So tall was he that his hat actually brushed the top of the doorway, and his breadth seemed to span it across from side to side. A large wrinkled face, marked with every evil passion, turned from one to the other of us, while his deep eyes, and thin nose, gave him the look of a fierce old bird of prey.

"Which of you is Holmes?" he asked.

"That's my name, sir, but you have the advantage of me," said my companion quietly.

"I am Dr. Grimesby Roylott, of Stoke Moran."

"Indeed, Doctor," said Holmes blandly. "Pray take a seat."

"I will do nothing of the kind. My stepdaughter has been here. I have traced her. What has she been saying to you?"

"It is a little cold for the time of year," said Holmes.

"What has she been saying to you?" screamed the old man furiously.

"But I have heard that the crocuses promise well," continued my companion.

"Ha! You put me off, do you?" said our new visitor, taking a step forward and shaking his hunting crop. "I know you, you scoundrel! You are Holmes the meddler."

My friend smiled.

"Holmes the busybody!"

Holmes chuckled. "Your conversation is most entertaining," said he. "When you go out close the door, for there is a draft."

"I will go when I have had my say. Don't you dare to meddle with my affairs. I know that Miss Stoner has been here – I traced her! I am a dangerous man to fall foul of! See here." He stepped swiftly forward, seized the poker, and bent it into a curve with his huge brown hands.

"See that you keep out of my grip," he snarled, and hurling the twisted poker into the fireplace, he strode out of the room.

"He seems very amiable," said Holmes, laughing. "I am not so bulky, but if he had remained I might have shown him that my grip was not much more feeble than his own." As he spoke he picked up the steel poker, and with a sudden effort straightened it out again.

"This gives zest to our investigation. And now,

Watson, we shall order breakfast, and afterwards I shall walk down to Doctors' Commons, where I hope to get some information that may help us in this matter."

It was nearly one o'clock when Sherlock Holmes returned. He held in his hand a sheet of blue paper, scrawled with notes and figures.

"I have seen the will of the deceased wife," said he. "The total income, which at the time of the wife's death was almost **£1,100**, is now not more than £750. Each daughter can claim an income of £250, in case of marriage. If both girls had married, Dr. Roylott would have had a mere pittance. Even one marriage would cripple him to a serious extent. My morning's work has proved that he has the very strongest motives for standing in the way of his stepdaughters' marriages. And now, Watson, this is too serious for dawdling, so if you are ready, we shall call a cab and drive to Waterloo. Please slip your revolver into your pocket."

£1,100
£ is the symbol for English money, called "pounds."

At Waterloo we were fortunate in catching a train for Leatherhead, where we hired a **trap** at the station inn, and drove for four or five miles through lovely Surrey lanes. My companion

TRAP
A two-wheeled carriage.

sat in front, his arms folded, his hat pulled down over his eyes, and his chin sunk upon his breast. Suddenly, however, he tapped me on the shoulder, and pointed. "Look there!" said he.

A heavily timbered park stretched up in a gentle slope, thickening into a grove at the highest point. From amidst the branches jutted out the grey gables and high roof of a mansion.

"Stoke Moran?" said he.

"Yes, sir, the house of Dr. Grimesby Roylott," remarked the driver.

"There is some building going on there," said Holmes. "That is where we are going."

"There's the village," said the driver, pointing to a cluster of roofs some distance to the left, "but if you want to get to the house, you'll find it shorter to take the footpath over the fields. There it is, where the lady is walking."

"And the lady, I fancy, is Miss Stoner," observed Holmes, shading his eyes. We got off, paid our fare, and the trap rattled back on its way to Leatherhead.

"Good afternoon, Miss Stoner," said Holmes. "You see we have been as good as our word."

WE GOT OFF AND PAID OUR FARE.

Our client hurried forward to meet us with a face that spoke her joy. "I have been waiting eagerly for you," she cried, shaking hands with us warmly. "All has turned out splendidly. Dr. Roylott has gone to town, and it is unlikely that he will be back before evening."

"We have had the pleasure of making the Doctor's acquaintance," said Holmes, and in a few words he sketched out what had occurred. Miss Stoner turned white as she listened.

"Heavens!" she cried, "he followed me?"

"So it appears."

"He is so cunning that I never know when I am safe from him. What will he say when he returns?"

"He must watch himself, for he may find that there is someone more cunning than himself on his track. Lock yourself from him tonight. If he is violent, we shall take you away to your aunt's. Now, we must make the best use of our time, so kindly take us at once to the rooms that we are to examine."

The building was of grey stone, with a high central portion and two curving wings. In one wing the windows were broken and blocked with wooden boards, while the roof was partly caved in. The central portion was in little better repair. The right-hand block was more modern, and the blinds in the windows, with the blue smoke curling up from the chimneys, showed that this was where the family resided. Holmes walked slowly up and down the lawn, examining the outsides of the windows.

"This, I take it, belongs to the room in which you used to sleep, the center one to your sister's, and the one next to the main building to Dr. Roylott's chamber?"

"Exactly so. But I am now sleeping in the middle one."

"Pending the alterations, as I understand. By the way, there does not seem to be any very pressing need for repairs at that end wall."

"There were none. I believe that it was an excuse to move me from my room."

"Ah! Now, on the other side runs the corridor from which these three rooms open. There are windows in it, of course?"

"Yes, but very small ones. Too narrow for anyone to pass through."

"As you both locked your doors at night, your rooms were unapproachable from that side. Now, would you have the kindness to go into your room and bar your shutters?"

Miss Stoner did so, and Holmes tried in every way to force the shutter open, but without success. "Hum!" said he, scratching his chin, "my theory certainly presents some difficulties. No one could pass these shutters if they were bolted. Well, we shall see if the inside throws any light upon the matter."

A small side door led into the corridor from which the three bedrooms opened. We passed at once to the one in which Miss Stoner was now sleeping, and in which her sister had met her fate. It was a homely little room, with a low ceiling and a gaping fireplace. A brown chest of drawers stood in one corner, a narrow bed in another, and a dressing-table on the left-hand side of the window. Holmes drew one of the chairs into a corner and sat silent, while his eyes travelled round and round and up and down, taking in every detail of the room.

"Where does that bell communicate with?" he asked at last, pointing to a thick bell-rope that hung down beside the bed.

"It goes to the housekeeper's room."

"It looks newer than the other things."

"Yes, it was put there a couple of years ago."

"Your sister asked for it, I suppose?"

"No, I never heard of her using it. We used always to get what we wanted for ourselves."

"Indeed, it seems unnecessary to put so nice a bell-rope there. You will excuse me for a few minutes while I examine this floor." He threw himself down upon his face and crawled swiftly backwards and forwards, examining closely the cracks between the boards. Then he did the same with the woodwork. Finally he walked over to the bed and spent some time staring at it, running his eyes up and down the wall. Then he took the bell-rope and gave it a brisk tug.

"Why, it's a dummy," said he. "It is not even attached to a wire. This is very interesting. It is fastened to a hook just above where the little opening of the ventilator is."

"How absurd! I never noticed that before."

"Very strange!" muttered Holmes. "There are one or two unusual points about this room. For example, what a fool a builder must be to open a vent into another room, when, with the same trouble, he might have the outside air!"

"That is also quite new," said the lady.

"Done about the same time as the bell-rope," remarked Holmes.

"Yes, there were several little changes carried out about that time."

"They have a most interesting character – dummy bell-ropes, and ventilators that do not ventilate. With your permission, Miss Stoner, we shall now carry our researches into the Doctor's room."

Dr. Roylott's chamber was larger than that of his stepdaughter, but was as plainly furnished. A bed, a

"WHAT'S IN HERE?" HE ASKED, TAPPING THE SAFE.

small wooden shelf full of books, an armchair beside the bed, a plain wooden chair against the wall, a round table, and a large iron safe were the principal things. Holmes slowly examined each of them with keen interest.

"What's in here?" he asked, tapping the safe.

"My stepfather's business papers."

"Oh! you have seen inside, then?"

"Only once, some years ago. I remember that it was full of papers."

"There isn't a cat in it, for example?"

"No. What a strange idea!"

"Well, look at this!" He took up a small saucer of milk that stood on the top of it.

"No, we don't keep a cat. But there is a cheetah and a baboon."

"Ah, yes, of course! Well, a cheetah is just a big cat. Yet a saucer of milk would not go very far in satisfying, I dare say. There is one point that I should wish to determine." He squatted down in front of the wooden chair and examined the seat of it with great attention.

"Thank you. That is quite settled," said he, rising. "Hullo! here is something interesting!"

The object that caught his eye was a small dog leash hung on one corner of the bed. It was curled upon itself and tied so as to make a loop.

"What do you make of that, Watson?"

"It's a common enough leash. But I don't know why it should be tied."

"That is not quite so common, is it? Ah, me! It's a wicked world, and when a clever man turns his brain to crime, it is the worst of all. I think that I have seen enough now, Miss Stoner, and, with your permission, we shall walk upon the lawn."

I had never seen my friend's face so grim, or his brow so dark, as it was when we turned from the scene of this investigation.

"It is very essential, Miss Stoner," said he, "that you absolutely follow my advice."

"I shall most certainly do so."

"The matter is too serious for any hesitation. Your life may depend upon your compliance."

"I assure you that I am in your hands."

"In the first place, Dr. Watson and I must spend the night in your room."

Both Miss Stoner and I gazed at him in astonishment.

"Yes, it must be so. Let me explain. I believe that that is the village inn over there?"

"Yes, that is the 'Crown.' "

"Your windows are visible from there?"

"Certainly."

"You must confine yourself to your room, on pretense of a headache, when your stepfather comes back. Then when you hear him retire for the night, you must open the shutters of your window, put your lamp there as a signal to us, and then withdraw to the room that you used to occupy. The rest you will leave in our hands."

"But what will you do?"

"We shall spend the night in your room and investigate this noise that has disturbed you."

"I believe, Mr. Holmes, that you have already made up your mind," said Miss Stoner.

"Perhaps I have."

"Then for pity's sake tell me what was the cause of my sister's death."

"I prefer clearer proofs before I speak."

"At least tell me whether my own thought is correct, if she died from some sudden fright."

"No, I do not think so. There was probably some more tangible cause. Now, Miss Stoner, we must leave you. If Dr. Roylott returned and saw us, our journey would be in vain. Goodbye, and be brave, for if you will do what I have told you, you may rest assured that we will soon drive away the dangers that threaten you."

Sherlock Holmes and I had no difficulty in engaging a bedroom and sitting room at the Crown Inn. They were on the upper floor, and we could see the inhabited wing of Stoke Moran Manor House. At dusk

"THEN FOR PITY'S SAKE TELL ME WHAT WAS THE CAUSE OF MY SISTER'S DEATH."

we saw Dr. Grimesby Roylott drive past, his huge form looming up beside the little figure of the lad who drove him. The boy had some difficulty in undoing the heavy iron gates, and we heard the hoarse roar of the Doctor's voice and saw the fury with which he shook his clenched fists at him. The trap drove on, and a few minutes later we saw a sudden light spring up among the trees as the lamp was lit in one of the sitting rooms.

"Do you know, Watson," said Holmes, as we sat together in the gathering darkness, "I have really some uneasiness as to taking you tonight. There is a distinct element of danger."

"Can I be of assistance?"

"Your presence might be invaluable."

"Then I shall certainly come."

"It is very kind of you."

"You speak of danger. You must have seen more in these rooms than was visible to me."

"No, but I fancy that I may have deduced a little more. I imagine that you saw all that I did."

"I saw nothing remarkable except the bell-rope, and what purpose that could answer I confess is more than I can imagine."

"You saw the ventilator, too?"

"Yes, but I do not think it is such an unusual thing to have a small opening between rooms. It was so small a rat could hardly pass through."

"I knew that we should find a ventilator before ever we came to Stoke Moran."

"My dear Holmes!"

"O, yes, I did. You remember Miss Stoner said that her sister could smell Dr. Roylott's cigar. Now, of course that suggests at once that there must be an opening between the two rooms. It could be only a small one, or it would have been remarked upon at the coroner's inquiry. Does not that strike you?"

"I cannot as yet see any connection."

"Did you observe anything very peculiar about that bed?"

"No."

"It was clamped to the floor. Did you ever see a bed fastened like that before?"

"I cannot say that I have."

"The lady could not move her bed. It must always be in the same relative position to the ventilator and to the rope."

"Holmes," I cried. "I see dimly what you are hitting at. We are only just in time to prevent some subtle and horrible crime."

"Subtle enough and horrible enough. When a doctor goes wrong he is the first of criminals. He has nerve and he has knowledge."

About nine o'clock the light among the trees was extinguished, and all was dark in the direction of the Manor House. Two hours passed slowly away, and then, suddenly, a single bright light shone out right in front of us.

"Our signal," said Holmes, springing up.

A moment later we were out on the dark road, a chill wind blowing in our faces. There was little difficulty in entering the grounds. Making our way among the trees, we reached the lawn, crossed it, and were about to enter through the window, when out from a clump of laurel bushes there darted what seemed to be a hideous and distorted child, who threw itself on the grass with writhing limbs and then ran swiftly across the lawn into the darkness.

"My God!" I whispered, "did you see it?"

Holmes was for the moment as startled as I. His

hand closed like a vice upon my wrist. Then he broke into a low laugh.

"That is the baboon," he murmured.

I had forgotten the strange pets. There was a cheetah, too; perhaps we might find it upon my shoulders at any moment. I felt easier in my mind when, after following Holmes's example and slipping off my shoes, I found myself inside the bedroom. My companion noiselessly closed the shutters, moved the lamp onto the table, and cast his eyes round the room. All was as we had seen it in the daytime. Then creeping up to me, he whispered into my ear again:

"The least sound would ruin our plans."

I nodded to show that I had heard.

"We must sit without a light. He would see it through the ventilator."

I nodded again.

"Do not go to sleep; your very life may depend upon it. Have your pistol ready. I will sit on the side of the bed, and you in that chair."

I took out my revolver and laid it on the corner of the table.

Holmes had brought a thin cane, and this he

placed upon the bed. By it he laid the box of matches and the stump of a candle. Then he turned down the lamp and we were in darkness.

Shall I ever forget that dreadful vigil? I could not hear a sound, and yet I knew that my companion sat open-eyed, within a few feet of me, in the same state of nervous tension in which I was myself. We waited in absolute darkness. From outside came the occasional cry of a night bird, and once a long, cat-like whine, which told us that the cheetah was at liberty.

Suddenly there was the momentary gleam of a light in the direction of the ventilator, which was succeeded by a strong smell of burning oil and heated metal. Someone in the next room had lit a lantern. I heard a gentle sound of movement, and then all was silent once more, though the smell grew stronger. For half an hour I sat with straining ears. Then suddenly another sound became audible – a gentle, soothing sound, like steam escaping from a kettle. The instant we heard it, Holmes sprang from the bed, struck a match, and lashed furiously with his cane at the bell-pull.

"You see it, Watson?" he yelled.

But I saw nothing. At the moment when Holmes

HOLMES LASHED FURIOUSLY WITH HIS CANE.

struck the light I heard a low, clear whistle, but the sudden glare in my weary eyes made it impossible for me to tell what it was my friend lashed so savagely. I could, however, see that his face was deadly pale, filled with horror and loathing.

He had ceased to strike and was gazing up at the ventilator, when there broke from the silence of the night the most horrible cry to which I have ever listened. It swelled up louder and louder, a yell of pain and fear and anger all mingled in the one dreadful shriek. It struck cold to our hearts, and I stood gazing at Holmes, and he at me, until the echoes of it died away.

"What can it mean?" I gasped.

"It means that it is all over," Holmes answered. "And perhaps for the best. Take your pistol, and we shall enter Dr. Roylott's room."

With a grave face he lit the lamp and led the way down the corridor. Twice he knocked at the door without any reply from within. Then he turned the handle and entered, I at his heels, with the cocked pistol in my hand.

A singular sight met our eyes. On the table stood a lantern with the shutter half open, throwing a brilliant beam of light upon the iron safe, the door of which was ajar. On the wooden chair sat Dr. Grimesby Roylott, clad in a long dressing gown. Across his lap lay the long leash we had noticed during the day. His chin was cocked upwards, and his eyes were fixed in a dreadful rigid stare at the corner of the ceiling. Round his brow he had a pe-

HE MADE NEITHER SOUND NOR MOTION.

culiar yellow band, with brownish speckles, which seemed to be bound tightly round his head. He made neither sound nor motion.

"The speckled band!" whispered Holmes.

I took a step forward. In an instant his strange headgear began to move, and there reared from his hair the squat diamond-shaped head and puffed neck of a loathsome serpent.

"It is a swamp adder!" cried Holmes – "the deadliest snake in India. He died within seconds of being bitten. Let us thrust this creature back into its den, and we can then remove Miss Stoner to some place of shelter and let the county police know what has happened."

As he spoke he drew the leash swiftly from the dead man's lap. Throwing the noose round the reptile's neck, he drew it from its perch, and, carrying it at arm's length, threw it into the iron safe, which he closed.

Such are the facts of the death of Dr. Grimesby Roylott, of Stoke Moran. The little I had yet to learn of the case was told to me by Sherlock Holmes as we traveled the next day.

"I had," said he, "come to an entirely incorrect conclusion, which shows how dangerous it is to reason from insufficient **data**. The presence of the gypsies, and the use of the word 'band,' put me on an entirely wrong scent. I reconsidered my position when it became clear that whatever danger threatened an occupant of the room could not come from the window or the door. My attention was drawn to this ventilator and the bell-rope. The discovery that this was a dummy, and that the bed was clamped to the floor, gave

DATA
Facts.

rise to the suspicion that the rope was a bridge for something passing through the hole and coming to the bed. The idea of a snake instantly occurred to me, and when I coupled it with my knowledge that the Doctor was furnished with creatures from India, I felt that I was on the right track. The idea of using a form of poison which could not be discovered by any chemical test was just such a one as would occur to a clever and ruthless man who had spent time in India. Then I thought of the whistle. Of course, he must recall the snake before the morning light revealed it to the victim. He trained it, probably by the use of the milk that we saw, to return to him when summoned. He would put it through the ventilator, certain that it would crawl down the rope and land on the bed. It might or might not bite the occupant; perhaps she might escape every night for a week, but sooner or later she must fall victim.

"I had come to these conclusions before ever I had entered his room. An inspection of his chair showed me that he had been in the habit of standing on it to reach the ventilator. The sight of the safe, the saucer of milk, and the loop of cord were enough to dispel any doubts that remained. The metallic clang heard by Miss

Stoner was caused by her stepfather hastily closing the door of his safe. Having made up my mind, you know the steps I took to put the matter to the proof. I heard the creature hiss, as no doubt you did also, and I instantly attacked it."

"Driving it through the ventilator."

"And also causing it to turn upon its master at the other side. The blows of my cane roused its temper, so that it flew upon the first person it saw. In this way I am indirectly responsible for Dr. Grimesby Roylott's death. I cannot say that it is likely to weigh heavily upon my conscience."

The Red-Headed League

I called upon my friend, Mr. Sherlock Holmes, and found him in deep conversation with an elderly gentleman with fiery red hair. I was about to withdraw, when Holmes pulled me abruptly into the room and closed the door.

"You could not possibly have come at a better time, my dear Watson," he said, cordially.

"I was afraid that you were engaged."

"So I am. Mr. Wilson, my dear friend Dr. Watson has been my helper in many of my most successful cases. I have no doubt that he will be of the utmost use to me in yours, also."

The stout gentleman half rose from his chair and gave a bob of greeting.

"Try the sofa," said Holmes, relapsing into his armchair. "I know, my dear Watson, that you share my love of all that is outside the routine of everyday life. Mr. Jabez Wilson here has called upon me this morning to begin a narrative that promises to be one of the most singular that I have listened to for some time. Perhaps, Mr. Wilson, you would kindly begin your narrative again. I ask you not merely because Dr. Watson has not heard the opening part, but also because the peculiar nature of the story makes me anxious to have every possible detail from your lips. In this instance the facts are, to the best of my belief, unique."

The portly Wilson puffed out his chest with pride and pulled a dirty newspaper from the pocket of his coat. As he glanced down the advertisement column, I tried to read the indications presented by his appearance.

I did not gain much by my inspection. Our visitor bore every mark of being an average British tradesman. He was obese, pompous and slow. He wore rather baggy grey-check trousers, a dirty black coat, unbuttoned, and a drab vest. A frayed top hat and a faded brown overcoat with a wrinkled velvet collar lay on a chair beside him. There was nothing remarkable about

MR. JABEZ WILSON

the man except his blazing red head, and the expression of extreme discontent on his features.

Sherlock Holmes shook his head with a smile as he noticed my questioning glances. "Beyond the obvious facts that he has done manual labor, that he takes snuff, that he is a **Freemason**, that he has been in China, and that he has done a considerable amount of writing lately, I can deduce nothing else."

FREEMASON
A member of an international secret fraternity.

Mr. Jabez Wilson started up in his chair, with his eyes upon my companion.

"How did you know all that, Mr. Holmes?" he asked. "How did you know, for example, that I did manual labor? It's as true as gospel. I began as a ship's carpenter."

"Your hands, my dear sir. Your right hand is larger than your left. You have worked with it, and the muscles are more developed."

"Well, the snuff, then, and Freemasonry?"

"I won't insult your intelligence by telling you how I read that, especially as you use an **arc and compass** breastpin."

ARC AND COMPASS
The symbols used by the Freemasons.

"Ah, I forgot that. But the writing?"

"What else can be indicated by that right cuff so very shiny for five inches, and the left one with the smooth patch by the elbow where you rest it upon the desk?"

"Well, but China?"

"The fish that you have tattooed above your right

wrist could only have been done in China. I have studied tattoo marks. That trick of staining the fish's scales pink is peculiar to China. When I see a Chinese coin hanging from your watch chain, the matter becomes simple."

Mr. Jabez Wilson laughed. "Well, I never! I thought at first you had done something clever, but I see that there was nothing in it after all."

"I begin to think, Watson," said Holmes, "that I make a mistake in explaining. My little reputation will be ruined if I am so candid. Can you not find the advertisement, Mr. Wilson?"

"Yes, I have got it now," he answered. "This is what began it all. Just read for yourself, sir."

I took the paper from him and read as follows:

TO THE RED-HEADED LEAGUE

On account of the bequest of the late Ezekiah Hopkins, of Lebanon, Penn., U.S.A., there is now another vacancy open which entitles a member of the League to a salary of four pounds a week for purely nominal services. All red-headed men who are sound in body and mind, and above the age of twenty-

> *one years, are eligible. Apply in person on Monday, at eleven o'clock, to Duncan Ross, at the offices of the League, 7 Pope's Court, Fleet Street.*

"What on earth does this mean?" I asked.

Holmes chuckled and wriggled in his chair, as was his habit when in high spirits. "It is a little off the beaten track, isn't it?" said he. "And now, Mr. Wilson, tell us all about yourself, your household, and the effect this advertisement had upon your fortunes. First make a note, Doctor, of the newspaper and the date."

"It is the *Morning Chronicle*, of April 27, 1890. Just two months ago."

"Very good. Now, Mr. Wilson?"

"Well, it is just as I have been telling you, Mr. Holmes," said Jabez Wilson. "I have a small pawnbroker's business. Lately it has barely given me a living. I used to keep two assistants, but now I keep only one. And I wouldn't be able to pay him, if he weren't willing to come for half wages, so as to learn the business."

"What is the name of this obliging youth?" asked Holmes.

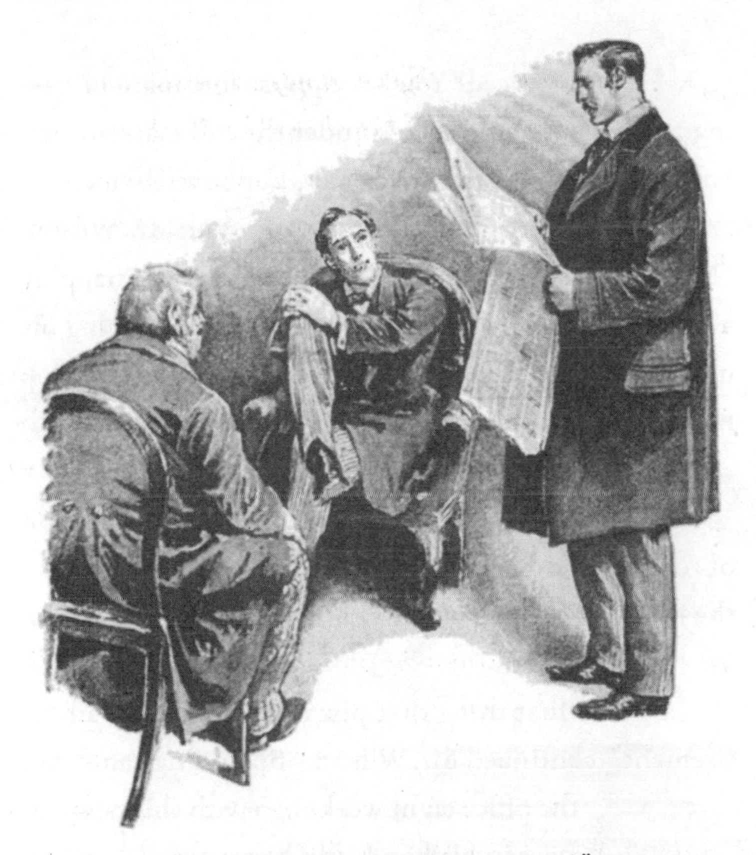

"WHAT ON EARTH DOES THIS MEAN?"

"His name is Vincent Spaulding, and he's not such a youth either. It's hard to say his age. I should not wish for a smarter assistant, Mr. Holmes. And I know very well that he could earn twice what I am able to give him. But, if he is satisfied, why should I put ideas in his head?"

"Why indeed? You seem most fortunate in having an employee who comes under the full market price. Your assistant is as remarkable as your advertisement."

"Oh, he has his faults, too," said Mr. Wilson. "Never was such a fellow for photography. Snapping away with a camera when he ought to be improving his mind, and then diving down into the cellar to develop his pictures. But on the whole, he's a good worker."

"He is still with you, I presume?"

"Yes, sir. He and a girl of fourteen, who does a bit of cooking and keeps the place clean – that's all I have in the house, for I am a widower and never had any family. We live very quietly.

"The first thing that **put us out** was that advertisement," continued Mr. Wilson. "Spaulding came into the office eight weeks ago with this newspaper in his hand, and he says:

PUT US OUT Caused us to do something.

" 'I wish to the Lord, Mr. Wilson, that I was a red-headed man.'

" 'Why?' I asked.

" 'Why,' says he, 'here's another vacancy on the League of the Red-Headed Men. It's worth a little fortune to any man who gets it. If my hair would only

"HERE'S ANOTHER VACANCY ON THE LEAGUE OF THE RED-HEADED MEN."

change color, here's a nice little job all ready for me to step into.'

" 'Why, what is it then?' I asked. You see, Mr. Holmes, I am a very stay-at-home man. I didn't know much of what was going on outside.

" 'Have you never heard of the League of the Red-Headed Men?' he asked, with his eyes open.

" 'Never.'

" 'Why, I wonder at that, for you are eligible yourself for one of the vacancies.'

" 'And what are they worth?' I asked.

" 'Oh, merely a couple of hundred a year, but the work is slight, and it need not interfere much with one's other occupations.'

"Well, that made me prick up my ears. An extra couple of hundred would have been very handy.

" 'Tell me all about it,' said I.

" 'Well,' said Spaulding, showing me the advertisement, 'you can see for yourself that the League has a vacancy, and there is the address where you should apply. As far as I can make out, the League was founded by an American millionaire, Ezekiah Hopkins, who was red-headed. When he died, he left his enormous fortune in the hands of trustees, with instructions to provide easy jobs to men whose hair is that color. From all I hear it is splendid pay, and very little to do.'

" 'But,' said I, 'millions of red-headed men would apply.'

" 'Not so many as you might think,' he answered. 'You see, it is really confined to Londoners and grown men. Mr. Hopkins came from London and he wanted to do the old town a good turn. I have heard it is no use applying if your hair is light red, or dark red, or anything but real, bright, blazing, fiery red. Now, if you apply, Mr. Wilson, you would just walk in.'

"My hair is of a very full and rich tint, so that it seemed to me that, if there was to be any competition in the matter, I stood as good a chance as any man. So we shut the business up and started off for the address given in the advertisement.

"I never hope to see such a sight as that again, Mr. Holmes. Every man who had a shade of red in his hair had tramped into the City to answer the advertisement. Every shade of color they were – straw, lemon, orange, brick, Irish-setter, liver, clay. But, as Spaulding said, there were not many who had the real vivid flame-colored tint. When I saw how many were waiting, I would have given it up, but Spaulding would not hear of it. He pushed and pulled until he got me through the crowd. We wedged in as well as we could and soon found ourselves in the office."

"Your experience has been a most entertaining one," remarked Holmes.

"There was nothing in the office but a couple of wooden chairs and a table, behind which sat a small man, with a head that was even redder than mine. He said a few words to each candidate as he came up, and then he always managed to find some fault that would disqualify them. However, when our turn came, the little man was more favorable to me. He closed the door as we entered, so that he might have a private word with us.

" 'This is Mr. Jabez Wilson,' said my assistant, 'and he is willing to fill a vacancy in the League.'

" 'And he is admirably suited for it,' the other answered. 'He has every requirement. I cannot recall when I have seen anything so fine.' He took a step backwards, cocked his head, and gazed at my hair until I felt quite bashful. Then suddenly he shook my hand and congratulated me.

" 'It would be an injustice to hesitate,' said he. 'You will, however, I am sure, excuse me for taking an obvious precaution.' With that he seized my hair in both

HE CONGRATULATED MR. WILSON WARMLY.

his hands and tugged until I yelled with the pain. 'There is water in your eyes,' said he, as he released me. 'All is as it should be. But we have to be careful, for we have twice been deceived by wigs.' He stepped over to the window, and shouted through it at the top of his voice that the vacancy was filled. A groan of disappointment came up from below, and the folk all trooped away.

" 'My name,' said he, 'is Mr. Duncan Ross, and I am myself one of the beneficiaries of the fund left by our noble benefactor. Are you a married man, Mr. Wilson? Have you a family?'

"I answered that I had not.

"His face fell immediately.

" 'Dear me!' he said gravely, 'I am sorry to hear you say that. The fund was, of course, intended to encourage the spread of red-heads. It is unfortunate that you should be a bachelor.'

"My face lengthened at this, Mr. Holmes, for I thought that I was not to have the vacancy after all. But after thinking it over for a few minutes, he said that it would be all right.

" 'In the case of another,' said he, 'the objection might be fatal, but we must stretch in favor of a man with such a head of hair. When shall you be able to enter your new duties?'

" 'Well, it is a little awkward, for I have a business already,' said I.

" 'Oh, never mind about that, Mr. Wilson!' said Spaulding. 'I shall look after that for you.'

" 'What would be the hours?' I asked.

" 'Ten to two.'

"Now a pawnbroker's business is mostly done in the evening, Mr. Holmes, so it would suit me well to earn a little in the mornings. Besides, I knew that my assistant was a good man, and would see to anything that turned up.

" 'That would suit me,' said I. 'And the pay?'

" 'Is four pounds a week.'

" 'And the work?'

" 'Is purely nominal.'

" 'What do you call purely nominal?'

" 'Well, you have to be in the office, or at least in the building, the whole time. If you leave, you forfeit your position forever. The will is very clear upon that point.'

" 'It's only four hours a day, and I should not think of leaving,' said I.

" 'No excuse will avail,' said Mr. Duncan Ross, 'neither sickness, nor business, nor anything else. There you must stay, or you lose your position.'

" 'And the work?'

" 'Is to copy out the *Encyclopedia Britannica*. Will you be ready tomorrow?'

" 'Certainly,' I answered.

" 'Then, goodbye, Mr. Jabez Wilson. Let me congratulate you on the important position you have been fortunate enough to gain.' He bowed and I went home pleased at my good fortune.

"Well, I thought over the matter all day, and by evening I was in low spirits again; I had persuaded myself that the whole affair must be some great hoax. It seemed improbable that anyone could make such a will, or that they would pay such a sum for doing anything so simple as copying out the *Encyclopedia Britannica*. Spaulding did what he could to cheer me up, but by bedtime I had reasoned myself out of the whole thing. However, in the morning I determined to have a look at it anyhow, so I started off to Pope's Court.

"Well, to my surprise and delight, everything was as right as possible. The table was ready for me, and Mr. Duncan Ross was there to see that I got straight to work. He started me off upon the letter A, and then he left me. He would drop in from time to time to see that all was right with me. At two o'clock he bade me good day, complimented me upon the amount that I had written, and locked the door after me.

"This went on day after day, Mr. Holmes, and on Saturday the manager gave me four golden sovereigns for my week's work. It was the same the next week, and the same the week after. Every morning I was there at ten, and every afternoon I left at two. Mr. Duncan Ross took to coming in only once a morning, and then, after a time, he did not come in at all. Still, I never dared to leave the room, for I was not sure when he might come, and the position suited me so well that I would not risk the loss of it.

"Eight weeks passed like this. I had written about Abbots, and Archery, and Armor, and Architecture, and Attica, and hoped that I might get on to the B's before very long. Then suddenly the whole business came to an end."

"To an end?"

"Yes, sir. This morning. I went to my work as usual, but the door was locked, with a little square of cardboard hammered onto the panel with a tack. Here, you can read for yourself."

THE DOOR WAS SHUT AND LOCKED.

He held up a piece of white cardboard, about the size of a sheet of paper. It read:

THE RED-HEADED LEAGUE
IS
DISSOLVED.
OCT. 9, 1890.

Sherlock Holmes and I surveyed this curt announcement and the sad face behind it, until we both burst out into a roar of laughter.

"I cannot see that there is anything very funny," cried our client. "If you can do nothing better than laugh at me, I can go elsewhere."

"No, no," cried Holmes, shoving him back into the chair from which he had half risen. "I really wouldn't miss your case for the world. It is most refreshingly unusual. But there is, if you will excuse me saying so, something just a little funny about it. Pray, what steps did you take when you found the card upon the door?"

"I was staggered, sir. I called at the offices nearby, but none of them seemed to know anything about it. Finally, I went to the landlord, who lives on the ground floor, and I asked him if he could tell me what had become of the Red-Headed League. He said that he had never heard of any such body. Then I asked him who Mr. Duncan Ross was. He answered that the name was new to him.

" 'Well,' said I, 'the gentleman at Room No. 4.'

" 'What, the red-headed man?'

" 'Yes.'

" 'Oh,' said he, 'his name was William Morris. He was an attorney, and he was using my room as a temporary convenience until his new offices were ready. He moved out yesterday.'

" 'Where could I find him?'

" 'At his new offices, 17 King Edward Street.'

"But when I got to that address it was a maker of artificial kneecaps, and no one in it had ever heard of either Mr. William Morris or Mr. Duncan Ross."

"And what did you do then?" asked Holmes.

"I went home, and I took the advice of my assistant. But he could only say that if I waited I might hear by mail. That was not quite good enough, Mr. Holmes. I did not wish to lose such a place without a struggle. So, as I had heard that you were good enough to give advice to poor folk, I came right to you."

"And you did very wisely," said Holmes. "Your case is a remarkable one, and I shall be happy to look into it. I think that graver issues hang from it than might at first sight appear."

"Grave enough!" said Mr. Jabez Wilson. "Why, I have lost four pounds a week."

"On the contrary," remarked Holmes, "you are richer by some thirty pounds, to say nothing of the knowledge you have gained on every subject that comes under the letter A. You have lost nothing."

"No, sir. But I want to find out about them, and who they are, and what their object was in playing this prank upon me."

"We shall clear up these points for you. First, one or two questions, Mr. Wilson. This assistant who first called attention to the advertisement – how long had he been with you?"

"About a month."

"How did he come?"

"In answer to an advertisement."

"Was he the only applicant?"

"No, I had a dozen."

"Why did you pick him?"

"Because he would come cheap."

"At half wages, in fact."

"Yes."

"What is he like, this Vincent Spaulding?"

"Small, stocky, very quick in his way, no hair on his face, though he's at least thirty. He has a white splash upon his forehead."

Holmes sat up in considerable excitement.

"I thought as much," said he. "Have you observed that his ears are pierced for earrings?"

"Yes, sir. He told me that a gypsy had done it for him when he was a lad."

"Hum!" said Holmes, sinking back in deep thought. "He is still with you?"

"Oh, yes, sir. I have only just left him."

"And has he attended to your business in your absence?"

"Nothing to complain of, sir. There's never very much to do of a morning."

"That will do, Mr. Wilson. I shall be happy to give you an opinion in a day or two."

"Well, Watson," said Holmes, when our visitor

HE CURLED HIMSELF UP IN HIS CHAIR.

had left us, "what do you make of it all?"

"I make nothing of it," I answered, frankly. "It is a most mysterious business."

"As a rule," said Holmes, "the more bizarre a thing is, the less mysterious it proves to be. It is your commonplace, featureless crimes which are really puzzling, just as a commonplace face is the most difficult to identify. But I must be prompt over this matter."

"What are you going to do then?" I asked.

"Smoke," he answered. He curled up in his chair, with his thin knees drawn up to his hawk-like nose, and there he sat with his eyes closed. I had come to the conclusion that he had dropped asleep, when he suddenly sprang out of his chair with the gesture of a man who had made up his mind.

"Sarasate, the great violinist, plays at the St. James's Hall this afternoon," he remarked. "What do you think, Watson? Could your patients spare you for a few hours?"

"I have nothing to do today."

"Then put on your hat. We can have some lunch on the way. Come along!"

We travelled by the **Underground** as far as Aldersgate; and a short walk took us to Saxe-Coburg Square, the scene of the story that we had listened to in the morning. Three gilt balls and a brown board with *"Jabez Wilson"* in white letters, upon a corner house, announced the place where our red-headed client carried on his business. Sherlock Holmes stopped and looked it all over. Then he walked

UNDERGROUND **Subway.**

THE DOOR WAS INSTANTLY OPENED.

slowly up the street and down again to the corner. Finally he returned to the pawnbroker's, and, having thumped upon the pavement with his walking stick two or three times, he went up to the door and knocked. It was opened by a bright-looking, clean-shaven young fellow, who asked him in.

"Thank you," said Holmes, "I only wished to ask you how you would go from here to the Strand."

"Third right, fourth left," answered the assistant promptly, closing the door.

"Smart fellow," observed Holmes as we walked away. "He is, in my judgment, the fourth smartest man in London. I have known something of him before."

"Evidently," said I, "Mr. Wilson's assistant counts for a good deal in this mystery of the Red-Headed League. I am sure you inquired your way merely in order that you might see him."

"Not him."

"What, then?"

"The knees of his trousers."

"And what did you see?"

"What I expected to see."

"Why did you beat the pavement?"

"My dear Doctor, this is a time for observation, not talk. Let us now explore the paths that lie behind Saxe-Coburg Square."

The road in which we found ourselves was one of the main arteries of the City. It was blocked with a stream of commerce and the sidewalks were black with hurrying pedestrians.

"Let me see," said Holmes, standing at the corner, "I should like just to remember the order of the houses here. It is a hobby of mine to have an exact knowledge of London. There is Mortimer's, the tobacconist, the little newspaper shop, the Coburg branch of the City and Suburban Bank, the Vegetarian Restaurant, and McFarlane's carriage depot. That carries us right on to the other block. And now, Doctor, we've done our work, so it's time we had some play. A sandwich, and a cup of coffee, and then off to violin-land, where there are no red-headed clients to vex us with their riddles."

My friend was an enthusiastic musician, being not only a very capable performer, but a composer of merit. All afternoon he sat in perfect happiness, gently waving his long thin fingers in time to the music, while his smiling face and his dreamy eyes were as unlike those

ALL AFTERNOON HE SAT IN PERFECT HAPPINESS.

of Holmes the sleuth as it was possible to conceive. As I knew well, he was never so formidable as when he had been lounging in his arm-chair amid his music. Then it was that the lust of the chase would suddenly come upon him, and that his brilliant reasoning power would rise.

"You want to go home, no doubt, Doctor," he remarked, as we emerged.

"Yes, it would be as well."

"And I have some business to do that will take some hours. This business at Coburg Square is serious. A considerable crime is being contemplated. I believe that we shall be in time to stop it. But today being Saturday complicates matters. I shall want your help tonight."

"At what time?"

"Ten will be early enough."

"I shall be at Baker Street at ten."

"Very well. And, I say, Doctor! There may be some danger, so kindly put your revolver in your pocket." He waved his hand and disappeared in an instant among the crowd.

I trust that I am not more dense than my neighbors, but I was always oppressed with a sense of my own stupidity in my dealings with Sherlock Holmes. Here I had heard what he had heard, I had seen what he had seen, and yet from his words it was evident that he saw clearly not only what had happened, but what was about to happen, while to me the whole business was still confused. As I drove home to my house, I thought over it all, from the extraordinary story of the red-headed copier of the *Encyclopedia* down to the visit to Saxe-Coburg Square, and the ominous words with which Holmes had parted from me. What was this nocturnal expedition, and why should I go armed? I had the hint from Holmes that this pawnbroker's assistant was a formidable man. I tried to puzzle it out, but gave it up in despair.

It was a quarter past nine when I started from home and made my way to Baker Street. Two hansoms were at the door, and as I entered I heard voices from above. On entering his room, I found Holmes with two men, one of whom I recognized as Peter Jones, the police agent. The other was a thin, sad-faced man, with a shiny hat.

"Ha! Our party is complete," said Holmes, buttoning his jacket and taking his heavy hunting crop from the rack. "Watson, I think you know Mr. Jones of Scotland Yard? Let me introduce you to Mr. Merryweather, who is to be our companion in tonight's adventure."

"We're hunting in couples again, Doctor, you see," said Jones.

"I hope a wild goose chase may not prove to be the end of our chase," observed Mr. Merryweather gloomily.

"You may place considerable confidence in Mr. Holmes, sir," said the police agent. "He has his own little methods, but once or twice he has been more nearly correct than the official force."

"If you say so, Mr. Jones, it is all right!" said the stranger. "Still, I miss my card game. It is the first Saturday night for twenty-seven years that I have not had my game."

"I think you will find, Mr. Merryweather," said Sherlock Holmes, "that you will play for a higher stake tonight than you have ever done yet, some thirty thousand pounds. And for you, Jones, it will be the man upon whom you wish to lay your hands."

"John Clay, the murderer, thief, and forger," Mr. Jones replied. "I would rather have handcuffs on him than on any criminal in London. He's a remarkable man. His grandfather was a Duke, and he himself has been to Oxford. He is cunning, and though we meet signs of him at every turn, we never know where to find the man himself. I've been on his track for years, and yet never set eyes on him."

"I hope that I may have the pleasure of introducing you tonight," said Holmes. "I've had one or two little turns also with Mr. John Clay, and I agree with you that he is at the head of his profession. It is past ten, however, and time we started. If you two will take the first hansom, Watson and I will follow in the second."

Sherlock Holmes lay back in the cab for the long drive, humming tunes he had heard in the afternoon.

"We are close now," my friend remarked. "This fellow Merryweather is a bank director and personally interested in the matter. I thought it as well to have Jones with us also. He is not a bad fellow, though an absolute imbecile in his profession. He has one virtue. He is as brave as a bulldog, and as tenacious as a lobster if he gets his claws upon anyone. Here we are."

We had reached the same street in which we had found ourselves in the morning. Our cabs were dismissed, and, following Mr. Merryweather, we passed down a narrow passage and through a side door, which he opened for us. Within there was a small corridor,

MR. MERRYWEATHER STOPPED TO LIGHT A LANTERN.

which ended in a very massive iron gate. This also was opened, and he led us down a flight of winding stone steps, which terminated at another formidable gate. Mr. Merryweather stopped to light a lantern and conducted us down a dark passage. Then he opened a third door, into a huge cellar, which was piled all around with crates and massive boxes.

"You are not very vulnerable from above," Holmes remarked, as he held up the lantern and gazed about him.

"Nor from below," said Mr. Merryweather, striking his stick upon the stone floor. "Why, dear me, it sounds quite hollow!" he remarked, looking up in surprise.

"I must ask you to be more quiet," said Holmes severely. "You have already imperiled the whole success of our expedition."

Mr. Merryweather perched on a crate, with an injured expression on his face, while Holmes fell upon his knees, and, with the lantern and magnifying lens, began to examine the cracks between the stones. A few seconds sufficed to satisfy him, for he sprang to his feet again.

"We have at least an hour before us," he remarked. "They can hardly take any steps until the good pawnbroker is safely in bed. Then they will not lose a minute, for the sooner they do their work the longer time they will have for their escape. We are, Doctor, in the cellar of one of the principal London banks. Mr. Merryweather is the chairman, and he will explain to you that there are reasons why the more daring criminals in London should take a considerable interest in this cellar at present."

"It is our French gold," whispered Merryweather. "We have had several warnings that an attempt might be made upon it. We had occasion some months ago to strengthen our resources, and we borrowed thirty thousand **napoleons** from the Bank of France. It has become known that we never unpacked the money, and that it is still lying in our cellar. The crate upon which I sit contains two thousand napoleons. Our reserve of gold is much larger at present than is usually kept in a single office, and the directors have been worried about it."

NAPOLEAN
Former gold coin of France.

"They were very well justified," observed Holmes. "I expect that within an hour, matters will come to a head. In the meantime, Mr. Merryweather, we must dim that lantern."

"And sit in the dark?"

"I am afraid so. The enemy's preparations have gone so far that we cannot risk the presence of a light. These are daring men, and, though we shall take them at a disadvantage, they may do us some harm, unless we are careful. I shall stand behind this crate, and you conceal yourself behind those. Then, when I flash upon them, close in swiftly. If they fire, Watson, shoot them down."

I placed my revolver, cocked, upon the top of the wooden case behind which I crouched. Holmes extinguished his lantern, leaving us in pitch darkness.

"They have one retreat," whispered Holmes, "back through the house into Saxe-Coburg Square. I hope you have done what I asked you, Jones?"

"An inspector and two officers wait at the front door."

"Then we have stopped all the holes. And now we must be silent and wait."

What a time it seemed! My limbs were weary and stiff. I feared to change my position, yet my nerves were worked up. Suddenly my eyes caught the glint of a light.

At first it was a small spark upon the stone pavement. Then it lengthened until it became a yellow line, and then a gash seemed to open and a hand appeared, a white, almost womanly hand. For a minute or more, its writhing fingers protruded out of the floor. Then it was withdrawn as suddenly as it appeared, and all was dark again except the single small spark, which marked a chink between the stones.

Its disappearance was but momentary. With a tearing sound, one of the broad stones turned over upon its side, and left a square, gaping hole, through which streamed the light of a lantern. Over the edge peeped a clean-cut, boyish face, which looked keenly about it, and then with a hand on either side of the opening, drew itself up. In an instant he stood at the side of the hole and was hauling after him a companion, small like himself, with very red hair.

"It's all clear," he whispered. "Have you the chisel and the bags? Great Scott! Jump, Archie, jump, and I'll swing for it!"

Sherlock Holmes had sprung out and seized the intruder by the collar. The other dived down the hole, and I heard the sound of tearing cloth as Jones clutched at his clothes. The light flashed upon the barrel of a revolver, but Holmes's hunting crop came down on the man's wrist, and the pistol clinked upon the stone floor.

"IT'S NO USE, JOHN CLAY."

"It's no use, John Clay," said Holmes blandly. "You have no chance at all."

"So I see," the other answered with the utmost

coolness. "I fancy that my pal is all right, though I see you have got his coattails."

"There are three men waiting for him at the door," said Holmes.

"Oh, indeed. I must compliment you."

"And I you," Holmes answered. "Your red-headed idea was very new and effective."

"You'll see your pal again presently," said Jones. "He's quicker at climbing down holes than I am. Just hold out while I fix the **derbies**."

DERBIES Handcuffs.

"I beg that you will not touch me with your filthy hands," remarked our prisoner, as the handcuffs clattered upon his wrists. "I have royal blood in my veins. Have the goodness when you address me to say 'sir' and 'please.' "

"All right," said Jones. "Well, would you please, sir, march upstairs, where we can get a cab to carry your highness to the police station?"

"That is better," said John Clay. He made a sweeping bow to the three of us and walked quietly off in the custody of the detective.

"Really, Mr. Holmes," said Mr. Merryweather, as we followed them from the cellar, "I do not know how the bank can thank you or repay you. There is no doubt that you have defeated one of the most determined attempts at bank robbery ever."

"I have had one or two little scores of my own to settle with Mr. John Clay," said Holmes. "I am amply repaid by having had an experience that is in many ways unique."

"You see, Watson," he explained in the early hours of the morning as we sat in Baker Street. "It was obvious from the first that the object of this advertisement of the League, and the copying of the *Encyclopedia*, must be to get this pawnbroker out of the way. The method was no doubt suggested to Clay's ingenious mind by the color of his accomplice's hair. The four pounds a week was a lure. And what was it to them, who were playing for thousands? They put in the advertisement. One rogue gets the pawnbroker to apply for it, and they secure his absence every morning in the week. From the time that I heard of the assistant coming for half-wages, it was obvious that he had a strong motive."

"But how did you guess the motive?"

"The man's business was small, and there was nothing in his house that could account for such elaborate preparations. It must then be something out of the house. What? I thought of the assistant's fondness for photography and his trick of vanishing into the cellar. The cellar! There was the end of this tangled clue. Then I made inquiries as to this mysterious assistant, and I found that I had to deal with one of the coolest and most daring criminals in London. He was doing something in the cellar that took many hours a day for months. What could it be? I could think of nothing except that he was running a tunnel to some other building.

"That was as far as I had gotten when we went to visit the scene. I surprised you by beating upon the pavement with my stick. I was checking to see whether the cellar stretched out in front or behind. It was not in front. Then I rang the bell, and, as I had hoped, the assistant answered it. We have had some skirmishes, but we had never set eyes on each other before. His knees were what I wished to see. You must have seen how worn, wrinkled and stained they were. It was from those hours of burrowing. The only remaining point was what they were burrowing for. I walked round the corner, saw that the City and Suburban Bank bordered on our friend's shop, and felt that I had solved my problem. When you drove home after the concert I called upon Jones and Merryweather."

"And how could you tell that they would make their attempt tonight?" I asked.

"When they closed their League offices that was a sign that they cared no longer about Mr. Jabez Wilson's presence. In other words, they had completed their tunnel. But it was essential that they should use it soon. It might be discovered, or the gold might be moved. Saturday would suit them better than any other day, as it would give them two days for their escape. For all these reasons I expected them to come tonight."

"You reasoned it out beautifully," I said.

"It saved me from boredom," he answered, yawning. "Alas, my life is one long effort to escape from the commonplaces of existence. These little problems help me to do so."

"And you are a benefactor of the race," said I.

He shrugged his shoulders. "Well, perhaps, after all, it is of some little use," he remarked.

The Adventure of the Engineer's Thumb

OF ALL THE PROBLEMS SUBMITTED TO SHERLOCK Holmes, that of Mr. Hatherley's thumb was so strange as to rank among the more remarkable – even if it gave my friend fewer opportunities for those deductive methods of reasoning by which he achieved such remarkable results.

It was in the summer of '89, not long after my marriage, that the events occurred that I am about to summarize. I had returned to my practice and had abandoned Holmes in his Baker Street rooms, although I continually visited him. My practice had steadily increased, and as I happened to live close to Paddington

Station, I got a few patients from among the officials. One of these, whom I had cured of a painful and lingering disease, was constantly advertising my virtues.

One morning, I was awakened by the maid tapping at the door, announcing that two men had come from Paddington and were waiting in the consulting room. I dressed hurriedly, for I knew by experience that railway cases were seldom trivial, and hastened downstairs. As I descended, my old friend, the guard, came out of the room, and closed the door tightly behind him.

"I've got him here," he whispered, jerking his thumb over his shoulder. "He's all right. I thought I'd bring him round myself; then he couldn't slip away. There he is, all safe and sound. I must go now, Doctor, I have my dooties, just the same as you." And off he went.

I entered my consulting-room and found a gentleman seated by the table. Round one of his hands he had a handkerchief wrapped, which was mottled all over with bloodstains. He was young, with a strong face, but he was exceedingly pale and looked like he was suffering from agitation.

"I am sorry to wake you, Doctor," said he. "But I have had a very serious accident during the night. I came in by train this morning, and on inquiring as to where I might find a doctor, a worthy fellow escorted me here. I gave the maid a card, but I see that she left it upon the side table."

I glanced at it. "Mr. Victor Hatherley, hydraulic engineer, 16A Victoria Street (3rd floor)."

"I regret that I have kept you waiting," said I, sitting down. "A night journey is a monotonous occupation."

"My night could not be called monotonous," said he. He laughed very heartily, with a ringing note, leaning back in his chair and shaking his sides. All my medical instincts rose up against that laugh.

"Stop it!" I cried. "Pull yourself together!" and I poured out some water from a carafe.

It was useless, however. He was off in one of those hysterical outbursts that come upon a strong nature when some great crisis is over. Presently he came to himself, very weary and blushing hotly.

"I have been making a fool of myself," he gasped.

"Not at all. Drink this!" I dashed some brandy into the water, and the color began to come back to his cheeks.

HE UNWOUND THE HANDKERCHIEF AND HELD OUT HIS HAND.

"That's better!" said he. "And now, Doctor, perhaps you would kindly attend to my thumb, or rather to the place where my thumb used to be."

He unwound the handkerchief and held out his hand. It gave even my hardened nerves a shudder to look at it. There were four fingers and a horrid red spongy surface where the thumb should have been. It had been hacked or torn right out from the roots.

"Good heavens!" I cried, "this is a terrible injury. It must have bled considerably."

"Yes, it did. I fainted when it was done; and I think I must have been senseless for a long time. When I came to, I found that it was still bleeding, so I tied one end of my handkerchief very tightly round the wrist and braced it up with a twig."

"Excellent! You should have been a surgeon."

"It is a question of hydraulics, you see, and came within my own specialty."

"This has been done," said I, examining the wound, "by a very heavy and sharp instrument."

"A thing like a cleaver," said he.

"An accident, I presume?"

"By no means."

"What, a murderous attack!"

"Very murderous indeed."

I sponged the wound, cleaned it, dressed it and, finally, covered it with bandages. He lay back without wincing, though he bit his lip from time to time.

"How is that?" I asked, when I had finished.

"Capital! Between your brandy and your bandage, I feel a new man. I was very weak, but I have had a good deal to go through."

"Perhaps you had better not speak of the matter. It is evidently trying to your nerves."

"Oh, no, not now. I shall have to tell my tale to the police; but, if it were not for the evidence of this wound, I should be surprised if they believed my story, for it is very extraordinary, and I have not much proof with which to back it up. Even if they believe me, the clues I can give them are so vague that I doubt justice will ever be done."

"If it is a problem that you desire to solve, I strongly recommend you come to my friend Mr. Sherlock Holmes before you go to the police."

"I have heard of that fellow," answered my visitor, "and I should be glad if he would take the matter up, though I must use the police as well. Would you give me an introduction to him?"

"I'll do better. I'll take you to him myself."

"I should be immensely obliged to you."

"We shall just be in time to have a little breakfast

HE SETTLED OUR NEW ACQUAINTANCE ON THE SOFA.

with him. Do you feel equal to it?"

"Yes. I shall not feel easy until I have told my story."

"Then I shall be with you in an instant." I rushed upstairs, explained the matter shortly to my wife, and in five minutes was in a cab, driving with my new acquaintance to Baker Street.

Sherlock Holmes was, as I expected, lounging about his sitting room in his dressing gown. He received us in his quietly genial fashion, ordered eggs, and joined us in a hearty meal. When it was concluded, he settled our new acquaintance upon the sofa and set a glass of brandy within his reach.

"It is easy to see that your experience has been no common one, Mr. Hatherley," said he. "Pray lie down there and make yourself at home. Tell us what you can, but stop when you are tired."

"Thank you," said my patient. "I am an orphan and a bachelor, residing alone in lodgings in London. By profession I am a hydraulic engineer, with considerable experience during the seven years that I was apprenticed to Venner & Matheson, the well-known firm. Two years ago, having come into a fair sum of money through my poor father's death, I decided to start in business for myself.

"I suppose that everyone finds his first independent start in business a dreary experience. To me it has been exceptionally so. During two years I have had only

COLONEL LYSANDER STARK

three consultations and one small job. Every day, from nine in the morning until four in the afternoon, I waited in my little den, until my heart began to sink, and I came to think I should never have any practice at all.

"Yesterday, however, my clerk entered to say there was a gentleman waiting to see me upon business. He brought a card, too, with the name of *'Colonel Lysander Stark'* engraved upon it. At his heels came the Colonel himself. I do not think that I have ever seen so thin a man. His whole face sharpened away into nose and chin. Yet this thinness seemed to be natural, and due to no disease, for his eye was bright, his step brisk, and his bearing assured. He was plainly but neatly dressed, and his age, I judge, would be near forty.

" 'Mr. Hatherley?'" said he, in a German accent. " 'You have been recommended to me as a man who is not only proficient in his profession, but is also capable of preserving a secret.' "

"I bowed, feeling as flattered as any young man would at such a greeting. 'May I ask who it was who gave me so good a reference?' I asked.

" 'Well, perhaps it is better that I should not tell you just at this moment. I have it from the same source that you are both an orphan and a bachelor, and you are residing alone in London.'

" 'That is quite correct,' I answered, 'but I cannot see how all this bears on my professional qualifications. I understood that it was on a professional matter that you wished to speak to me?'

" 'You will find that all I say is to the point. I have a professional commission for you, but absolute secrecy is essential – absolute secrecy, you understand, and of course we may expect that more from a man who lives alone than from one who lives in the bosom of his family.'

" 'If I promise to keep a secret,' said I, 'you may absolutely depend upon my doing so.'

"He looked hard at me as I spoke, and I have never seen so suspicious and questioning an eye.

" 'You do promise, then?' said he at last.

" 'Yes, I promise.'

" 'Absolute and complete silence, before, during, and after? No reference to the matter at all, either in word or writing?'

" 'I have already given you my word.'

" 'Very good.'

"He drew up his chair very close to mine, and

began to stare at me again with the same questioning and thoughtful look.

"A feeling of repulsion and fear had begun to rise within me at the antics of this fleshless man.

" 'I beg that you will state your business, sir,' said I; 'my time is of value.' Heaven forgive me that last sentence, but the words came to my lips.

" 'How would fifty guineas for a night's work suit you?' he asked.

" 'Most admirably.'

" 'I say a night's work. But an hour's would be nearer the mark. I simply want your opinion about a hydraulic stamping machine that has gotten out of gear. If you show us what is wrong, we shall set it right ourselves. What do you think?'

" 'The work appears to be light, and the pay generous.'

" 'Precisely so. We shall want you to come tonight by the last train to Eyford, in Berkshire. It is a little place near the borders of Oxfordshire. There is a train from Paddington that would bring you in there at about eleven fifteen. I shall come down in a carriage to meet you.'

" 'There is a drive, then?'

" 'Yes, our little place is in the country. It is a good seven miles from Eyford station.'

" 'Then we can hardly get there before midnight. I suppose there would be no chance of a train back. I should be forced to stop for the night.'

" 'Yes, we could easily give you a **shakedown**.'

" 'That is very awkward. Could I not come at some more convenient hour?'

SHAKEDOWN A makeshift bed.

" 'We judge it best that you should come late. It is to recompense you for any inconvenience that we are paying you, an unknown man, a fee that would buy an opinion from the very heads of your profession. Of course, if you would like to get out of this business, there is time to do so.'

"I thought of the fifty guineas, and of how very useful they would be to me. 'Not at all,' said I; 'I should like, however, to understand a little more clearly what it is that you wish me to do.'

" 'Quite so. It is very natural that the pledge of secrecy aroused your curiosity. I have no wish to commit you to anything without your having it all laid before you. I suppose that we are absolutely safe from eavesdroppers?'

" 'Entirely.'

" 'The matter stands thus. You may be aware that **fuller's earth** is a valuable product, and that it is only found in one or two places in England?'

FULLER'S EARTH
A clay used in manufacturing processes.

" 'I have heard so.'

" 'Some little time ago I bought a small place within ten miles of Reading. I was fortunate to discover that there was a deposit of fuller's earth in one of my fields. On examining it, however, I found that this deposit formed a link between two very much larger ones – both of them in the grounds of my neighbors. These good people did not know that their land contained that which was quite as valuable as a gold mine. Naturally, it was to my interest to buy their land before they discovered its true value; but I had no money by which I could do this. I took a few of my friends into the secret, however, and they suggested that we should secretly work our own little deposit, and in this way earn the money to buy the neighboring fields. This we have now been doing for some time, and to help us in our operations we erected a hydraulic press. This press, as I have already explained, has gotten out of order, and we wish your advice. We guard our secret very jealously, however. If it became known that we had hydraulic engineers coming to our little house, it would soon rouse suspicion. That is why I have made you promise me that you will not tell a human being that you are going to Eyford tonight. I hope that I make it all plain?'

" 'The only point that I could not quite understand,' said I, 'was what use you could make of a hydraulic press in excavating fuller's earth, which, as I understand, is dug out from a pit.'

" 'Ah!' said he carelessly, 'we have our own process. We compress the earth into bricks, so as to remove them without revealing what they are. But that is a mere detail. I have taken you fully into my confidence, now, Mr. Hatherley, and I have shown you how I trust you.' He rose as he spoke. 'I shall expect you, then, at Eyford, at 11:15.'

" 'I shall certainly be there.'

" 'And not a word to a soul.' He looked at me with a last long, questioning gaze, and then he hurried from the room.

"Well, when I came to think it all over I was much astonished at this sudden commission. On the one hand, of course, I was glad, for the fee was at least

"NOT A WORD TO A SOUL!"

ten times what I should have asked had I set a price on my own services, and this order might lead to other ones. On the other hand, my patron had made an unpleasant impression upon me, and I could not think that his explanation was sufficient to explain the necessity for my coming at midnight, and his extreme anxiety least I should tell anyone of my errand. However, I threw my fears to the winds, ate a hearty supper, drove to Paddington, and started off, having obeyed to the letter the order to hold my tongue.

"I was in time for the last train to Eyford, and I reached the little station after eleven o'clock. I was the only passenger who got out there, and there was no one upon the platform. As I passed out the gate, however, I found my acquaintance of the morning waiting in the shadow. Without a word he grasped my arm and hurried me into a carriage. He drew up the windows on either side and away we went, as hard as the horse could go."

"One horse?" interjected Holmes.

"Yes, only one."

"Did you observe the color?"

"Yes, it was a chestnut."

"Tired-looking or fresh?"

"Oh, fresh and glossy."

"Thank you. Pray continue your tale."

"We drove for at least an hour. Colonel Stark had said that it was only seven miles, but I think that it must have been nearer twelve. He sat in silence all the time, and I was aware that he was looking at me with great intensity. The country roads seemed to be not very good, for we lurched and jolted terribly. I tried to look out of the windows to see something of where we were, but they were made of frosted glass, and I could make out nothing except an occasional blur of passing light. Now and then I hazarded some remark to break the boredom of the journey, but the Colonel answered only in grunts. At last, however, the carriage came to a stand. Colonel Lysander Stark sprang out, and, as I followed, pulled me swiftly on a porch in front of us. We stepped, as it were, right out of the carriage and into the hall, so that I failed to catch even the most fleeting glance of the front of the house. The instant that I had crossed the threshold the door slammed heavily behind us, and I heard faintly the rattle of the wheels as the carriage drove away.

"It was pitch dark in the house. The Colonel fumbled about looking for matches and muttering under his breath. Suddenly a door opened at the other end of the passage, and a long, golden bar of light shot out in our direction. A woman appeared with a lamp in her hand, peering at us. I could see that she was pretty. She spoke a few words in a foreign tongue as though asking a question, and when my companion answered gruffly, she gave such a start that the lamp nearly fell from her hand. Colonel Stark went up to her, whispered something, and then, pushing her back into the room from whence she had come, he walked towards me again with the lamp.

" 'Perhaps you will have the kindness to wait in this room for a few minutes,' said he, throwing open another door. It was a little plain room, with a round table in the center, on which several German books were scattered. 'I shall not keep you waiting,' said he, and vanished into the dark.

"I glanced at the books upon the table, and in spite of my ignorance of German, I could see that two of them were treatises on science, the other being poetry. Then I walked across to the window, hoping that I might catch some glimpse of the countryside, but an oak shutter was folded across it. It was a wonderfully silent house. There was an old clock ticking loudly somewhere, but otherwise everything was deadly still. An uneasiness began to steal over me. Who were these German people, and what were they doing living in this strange, out-of-the-way place? And where was the place? I was ten miles or so from Eyford, that was all I knew. I paced the room, humming a tune under my breath to keep up my spirits, and feeling that I was thoroughly earning my fifty-guinea fee.

"Suddenly, the door of my room swung slowly open. The woman was standing in the opening, the darkness of the hall behind her, the yellow light from my lamp on her eager, beautiful face. I could see that she was sick with fear, and the sight sent a chill to my own heart. She held up one shaking finger to warn me to be silent, and she shot a few words of broken English at me, her eyes glancing back into the gloom behind her.

" 'I would go,' said she, trying hard to speak calmly. 'There is no good for you to do.'

" 'But, madam,' said I, 'I cannot possibly leave until I have seen the machine.'

" 'It is not worth your while to wait,' she went on. 'You can pass through the door; no one hinders.'

"GET AWAY FROM HERE BEFORE IT IS TOO LATE."

And then, seeing that I smiled and shook my head, she made a step forward, with her hands together. 'For the love of Heaven!' she whispered, 'get away before it is too late!'

"But I am somewhat headstrong by nature. I thought of my fifty-guinea fee, of my wearisome journey, and the unpleasant night that seemed to be before me. Was it all for nothing? Why should I slink away without having carried out my commission, and without the payment that was my due? With a stout bearing, therefore, I declared my intention of remaining where I was. She was about to renew her pleas when a door slammed, and the sound of several footsteps was heard upon the stairs. She listened for an instant, threw up her hands with a despairing gesture, and vanished as noiselessly as she had come.

"The newcomers were Colonel Lysander Stark and a short thick man with a beard growing out of his double chin, who was introduced to me as Mr. Ferguson.

" 'This is my secretary and manager,' said the Colonel. 'By the way, I was under the impression that I left this door shut. I fear that you have felt the draught.'

" 'On the contrary,' said I, 'I opened the door myself, because I felt the room to be a little close.'

"He shot one of his suspicious glances at me. 'Perhaps we had better proceed to business, then,' said he. 'Mr. Ferguson and I will take you to see the machine.'

" 'I had better put my hat on, I suppose.'

" 'Oh no, it is in the house.'

" 'What, you dig fuller's earth in the house?'

" 'No, no. This is only where we compress it. But never mind that! All we wish you to do is examine the machine and to let us know what is wrong with it.'

"We went upstairs together, the Colonel first with the lamp, the fat manager and I behind him. It was a mysterious old house, with passages, narrow winding staircases, and little low doors. There were no carpets, no signs of any furniture above the ground floor, and plaster was peeling off the walls. I tried to put on an unconcerned air, but I had not forgotten the warnings of the lady, even though I disregarded them. I kept a keen eye on my two companions. Ferguson seemed a gloomy, silent man, but I could see from the little he said that he was at least a fellow Englishman.

"Colonel Lysander Stark stopped at last before a low door, which he unlocked. Within was a small square room, in which the three of us could hardly fit at one time. Ferguson remained outside, and the Colonel ushered me in.

" 'We are now,' said he, 'actually within the hydraulic press, and it would be particularly unpleasant for us if anyone were to turn it on. The ceiling of this small chamber is really the end of the descending piston, and it comes down with the force of many tons upon this metal floor. There are small columns of water outside that receive the force, and which transmit and multiply it in the manner that is familiar to you. The machine goes readily enough, but it has lost a little of its force. Perhaps you will look it over and show us how we can set it right.'

"I took the lamp from him, and I examined the machine very thoroughly. It was indeed gigantic and was capable of exercising enormous pressure. When I pressed down the levers that controlled it, I knew at once by the whishing sound that there was a slight leakage. An examination showed that one of the rubber bands around the end of a driving-rod had shrunk so as not quite to fill the socket along which it worked. This was clearly the cause of the loss of power, and I pointed it out to my companions, who asked several practical questions as to how they should set it right. When I had made it clear to them, I returned to the main chamber of the machine and took a good look at it to satisfy my curiosity. It was obvious that the story of the fuller's earth was a fabrication, for it would be absurd to suppose that so powerful an engine could be designed for so small a purpose. The walls were of wood, but the floor consisted of a large iron trough, and I could see a crust of metallic deposit all over it. I was scraping at it to see exactly what it was, when I heard an exclamation in German, and saw the ghostly face of the Colonel looking down at me.

" 'What are you doing there?' he asked.

"I felt angry at having been tricked by so elaborate a story as that he had told me. 'I think that I would be better able to advise you as to your machine,' said I, 'if I knew what the exact purpose was for which it was used.'

"The instant that I uttered the words I regretted the rashness of my speech. A sinister light sprang up in his grey eyes.

" 'Very well,' said he, 'you shall know all about the machine.' He took a step backward, slammed the door, and turned the key in the lock. I rushed towards it

I RUSHED TO THE DOOR.

and pulled at the handle, but it was secure and did not give in to my kicks and shoves. 'Hallo!' I yelled. 'Colonel! Let me out!'

"And then suddenly in the silence I heard the clank of the levers and the swish of the leaking cylinder. He had set the engine at work. The lamp still stood upon the floor where I had placed it. By its light I saw that the black ceiling was coming down on me, slowly, jerkily, but, as none knew better than myself, with a force that must grind me to a shapeless pulp. I threw myself, screaming, against the door. I begged the Colonel to let me out, but the remorseless clanking of the levers drowned my cries. The ceiling was only a foot or two above my head, and with my hand I could feel its hard rough surface. Then it flashed through my mind that the pain of my death would depend on the position in which I met it. If I lay on my face the weight would come upon my spine. I shuddered to think of that dreadful snap. Easier the other way, perhaps, and yet had I the nerve to lie and look up at that deadly black shadow wavering down upon me? Already I was unable to stand erect, when my eye caught something that brought a gush of hope back.

"Though the floor and ceiling were of iron, the walls were of wood. As I gave a last hurried glance around, I saw a thin line of yellow light between two of the boards, which broadened as a small panel was pushed backwards. I could hardly believe that here was indeed a door that led away from death. I threw myself through it and lay half fainting upon the other side. The panel had closed again behind me, but the clang of the two slabs of metal told me how narrow had been my escape.

"I was recalled to myself by a frantic plucking at my wrist. I found myself lying on the stone floor of a narrow corridor. A woman bent over me and tugged at me with her left hand, while she held a candle in her right. It was the same friend whose warning I had so foolishly rejected.

" 'Come!' she cried breathlessly. 'They will be here in a moment. They will see that you are not there. Do not waste precious time, but come!'

"This time, I did not scorn her advice. I staggered to my feet and ran with her along the corridor and down a winding stair. This led to another broad passage, and, just as we reached it, we heard the sound of running feet and the shouting of two voices from the floor on which we were, and from the one beneath. My guide stopped and looked about her. Then she threw open a door to a bedroom, through the window of which the moon was shining brightly.

" 'It is your only chance,' said she. 'It is high, but it may be that you can jump it.'

"As she spoke, a light sprang into view at the further end of the passage, and I saw the lean figure of Colonel Lysander Stark rushing forward with a lantern in one hand and a butcher's cleaver in the other. I rushed across the bedroom, flung open the window, and looked out. How quiet and sweet and wholesome the garden looked in the moonlight, and it could not be more than thirty feet down. I clambered out upon the sill, but I hesitated to jump, so I could hear what passed between my savior and the ruffian who pursued me. If she were ill-used, then at any risk I was determined to go back to her assistance. The thought had hardly flashed through my mind before he was at the door, pushing his way past her. She threw her arms round him and tried to hold him back.

" 'Fritz! Fritz!' she cried in English, 'remember your promise after the last time. You said it would not happen again. He will be silent!'

MY HANDS WERE ACROSS THE SILL WHEN HIS BLOW FELL.

" 'You are mad, Elise!' he shouted, struggling to break away from her. 'You will be the ruin of us. He has seen too much.' He dashed her to one side, and, rushing to the window, cut at me with his heavy weapon. I was hanging with my hands across the sill when his blow fell. I was conscious of a dull pain, my grip loosened, and I fell into the garden below.

"I was shaken, but not hurt by the fall; so I picked myself up and rushed off among the bushes as hard as I could run. I understood that I was far from being out of danger yet. Suddenly, however, as I ran, a deadly dizziness came over me. I glanced at my hand, which was throbbing painfully, and, for the first time, saw that my thumb had been cut off. Blood was pouring from my wound. I tried to tie my handkerchief round it, but there came a buzzing in my ears, and I fell in a dead faint among the bushes.

"How long I remained unconscious I cannot tell. It must have been a long time, for a bright morning was breaking when I came to myself. My clothes were all wet with dew, and my coat-sleeve was drenched with blood. The pain recalled in an instant my night's adventures, and I sprang to my feet with the feeling that I might hardly yet be safe from my pursuers. But, to my astonishment, neither house nor garden were to be seen. I had been lying in an angle of the hedge close by the road, and just a little lower down was the very train station at which I had arrived the previous night.

"Half dazed, I went into the station and asked about the morning train. There would be one to Reading in less than an hour. I asked the porter whether he had ever heard of Colonel Lysander Stark. The name was strange to him. Was there a police station nearby? There was one about three miles off.

"It was too far for me to go, weak as I was. I determined to wait until I got back to town before telling my story to the police. I went first to have my wound dressed, and then the doctor was kind enough to bring me along here. I put the case in your hands, and I shall do exactly as you advise."

We sat in silence for some time. Then Sherlock Holmes pulled from the shelf one of the books in which he placed his newspaper cuttings.

"Here is an advertisement that will interest you," said he. "It appeared in all the papers about a year ago. Listen to this: – 'Lost on the 9th inst., Mr. Jeremiah

Hayling, aged 26, a hydraulic engineer. Left his lodgings at ten o'clock at night, and has not been heard of since. Was dressed in,' etc. etc. Ha! That represents the last time the Colonel needed his machine overhauled, I fancy."

"Good heavens!" cried my patient. "Then that explains what the girl said."

"Undoubtedly. It is clear that the Colonel was a cool and desperate man, who was absolutely determined that nothing should stand in the way of his little game. Every moment now is precious, so, if you feel equal to it, we shall go down to Scotland Yard at once before starting for Eyford."

Three hours or so afterwards we were all in the train together. There were Sherlock Holmes, the hydraulic engineer, Inspector Bradstreet of Scotland Yard, a plain-clothes officer, and myself. Bradstreet had spread a map of the country out upon the seat and was busy with his compass drawing a circle with Eyford for its center.

"There you are," said he. "That circle is drawn at a radius of ten miles from the village. The place we want must be somewhere near that line. You said ten miles, I think, sir?"

"It was an hour's good drive."

"And you think that they brought you back all that way when you were unconscious?"

"They must have. I have a confused memory, too, of being lifted and conveyed somewhere."

"What I cannot understand," said I, "is why they should have spared you when they found you lying fainting in the garden."

"Oh, we shall soon clear up all that," said Bradstreet. "Well, I have drawn my circle, and I only wish I knew at what point upon it the folk that we are in search of are to be found."

"I think I could lay my finger on it," said Holmes quietly.

"Really, now!" cried the inspector, "you have formed your opinion! Come now, we shall see who agrees with you. I say it is south, for the country is more deserted there."

"And I say east," said my patient.

"I am for the west," remarked the plain-clothes man. "There are quiet little villages up there."

"And I am for the north," said I; "because there are no hills there, and our friend says that he did not notice the carriage go up any."

"Come," said the inspector, laughing, "who do you give your casting vote to?"

"You are all wrong."

"But we can't all be."

"Oh, yes, you can. This is my point," he placed his finger on the center of the circle. "This is where we shall find them."

"But the twelve mile drive?" gasped Hatherley.

"Six out and six back. Nothing simpler. You say yourself that the horse was fresh and glossy when you got in. How could it be that, if it had gone twelve miles over heavy roads?"

"Indeed it is a likely enough ruse," observed Bradstreet thoughtfully. "Of course there can be no doubt as to the nature of this gang."

"None at all," said Holmes. "They are counterfeiters on a large scale; they have used the machine to form the metal mixture that has taken the place of silver."

"We have known for some time that a clever gang was at work," said the inspector. "They have been turning out half-crowns by the thousand. We even traced them as far as Reading, but could get no further. But now, thanks to this lucky chance, I think that we have got them."

But the inspector was mistaken, for those criminals were not destined to fall into the hands of justice. As we rolled into Eyford station we saw a gigantic column of smoke that streamed up from behind a small clump of trees in the neighborhood and hung over the landscape.

"A house on fire?" asked Bradstreet.

"Yes, sir," said the stationmaster.

"When did it break out?"

"I hear that it was during the night, sir, but it has got worse, and the whole place is in a blaze."

"Whose house is it?"

"Dr. Becher's."

"Tell me," broke in the engineer, "is Dr. Becher a German, very thin, with a long nose?"

The stationmaster laughed. "No, sir, Dr. Becher is an Englishman, and there isn't a man in the parish who has a better lined waist. But he has a gentleman staying with him, a patient as I understand, who is a foreigner, and he looks as if a little good beef would do him no harm."

WE SAW A GIGANTIC COLUMN OF SMOKE.

The stationmaster had not finished his speech before we were all hastening in the direction of the fire. The road topped a low hill, and there was a great white building in front of us, spouting fire at every window.

"That's it!" cried Hatherley, in intense excitement. "There is the gravel drive, and there are the rose bushes where I lay. That second window is the one that I jumped from."

"Well, at least," said Holmes, "you have had your revenge upon them. There can be no question that it was your oil lamp that, when it was crushed in the press, set fire to the wooden walls, though no doubt they were too excited in the chase after you to observe it at the time. Now keep your eyes open in this crowd for your friends of last night, though I very much fear that they are a good hundred miles off by now."

And Holmes's fears came to be realized, for from that day to this no word has ever been heard either of the beautiful woman, the sinister German, or the gloomy Englishman.

The firemen had been much perturbed at the strange arrangements that they found within, and still more so by discovering a newly severed human thumb upon a window-sill of the second floor. About sunset, however, their efforts were at last successful, and they subdued the flames, but not before the roof had fallen in, and the whole place reduced to ruin. Large masses of nickel and tin were discovered stored in an outhouse.

How our hydraulic engineer had been moved from the garden to the spot where he recovered his senses might have remained forever a mystery were it not for the soft ground, which told us a very plain tale. He had evidently been carried down by two persons, one of whom had remarkably small feet, and the other unusually large ones. It was probable that the silent Englishman, being less bold or less murderous than his companion, had assisted the woman to bear the unconscious man out of danger.

"Well," said our engineer, as we took our seats to return to London, "it has been a pretty business for me! I have lost my thumb, and I have lost a fifty-guinea fee, and what have I gained?"

"Experience," said Holmes, laughing. "Indirectly it may be of value, you know. You have only to put it into words to gain the reputation of being excellent company for the remainder of your existence."

The Adventure of the Blue Carbuncle

I HAD CALLED UPON MY FRIEND SHERLOCK HOLMES on the second morning after Christmas to wish him the compliments of the season. He was lounging upon the sofa in a purple dressing gown, with a pile of crumpled morning papers near. Beside the couch was a wooden chair, and on it hung a very seedy felt hat, much the worse for wear. Objects lying upon the seat of the chair suggested Holmes had been studying the hat.

"You are engaged," said I; "perhaps I interrupt you."

"Not at all. I am glad to have a friend with whom I can discuss my results. The matter is a perfectly trivial

ON THE CHAIR HUNG A VERY SEEDY FELT HAT.

one, but there are points in it that are interesting, and even instructive."

I seated myself in his armchair and warmed my hands before his crackling fire. A sharp frost had set in, and the windows were thick with ice crystals. "I suppose," I remarked, "that, homely as it looks, this thing has some story linked to it – that it will guide you in the solution of some mystery, and the punishment of some crime."

"No, no. No crime," said Sherlock Holmes, laughing. "Only one of those whimsical little incidents that will happen when you have four million human beings all jostling each other within the space of a few square miles. Do you know Peterson, the commissionaire?"

"Yes."

"It is to him that this trophy belongs."

"It is his hat."

"No, no; he found it. Its owner is unknown. Look upon it, not as a battered **billycock**, but as an intellectual problem. It arrived upon Christmas morning, with a good fat goose, which is, I have no doubt, roasting at this moment in front of Peterson's fire. The facts are these. About four o'clock on Christmas morning, Peterson, who, as you know, is a very honest fellow, was returning from some small party and was making his way home down Tottenham Court Road. In front of him he saw a tallish man, walking with a slight stagger, and carrying a white goose slung over his shoulder. As he reached the corner of Goodge Street a row broke out between this stranger

BILLYCOCK
A man's felt hat.

THE THUGS FLED AT THE APPEARANCE OF PETERSON.

and a group of thugs. One of them knocked off the man's hat, at which he raised his walking stick to defend himself, and, swinging it over his head, smashed the shop window behind him. Peterson rushed forward to protect the stranger from his assailants, but the man, shocked at seeing an official-looking person in uniform rushing towards him, dropped his goose, took to his heels, and vanished amid the streets. The thugs also fled at the appearance of Peterson, so that he was left in possession of the spoils of victory, this battered hat and a most impressive Christmas goose."

"Which surely he restored to their owner?"

"There lies the problem. It is true that 'For Mrs. Henry Baker' was printed upon a small card that was tied to the bird's leg, and it is also true that the initials 'H.B.' are legible upon the lining of this hat; but, as there are thousands of Bakers and hundreds of Henry Bakers in this city, it is not easy to restore lost property to any one of them."

"What, then, did Peterson do?"

"He brought both hat and goose to me on Christmas morning, knowing that even the smallest problems interest me. The goose we retained until there were signs that it should be eaten without delay. Peterson has carried it off therefore to fulfill the ultimate destiny of a goose, while I continue to retain the hat of the unknown gentleman who lost his Christmas dinner."

"Did he not advertise?"

"No."

"Then, what clue could you have as to his identity?"

"Only as much as we can deduce."

"From his hat?"

"Precisely."

"But you are joking. What can you gather from this old battered felt?"

"Here is my lens. You know my methods. What can you gather as to the individuality of the man who has worn this article?"

I took the tattered object in my hands, and turned it over. It was a very ordinary black hat of the usual round shape, hard and much the worse for wear. The lining had been of red silk, but was discolored. There was no maker's name; but, as Holmes had remarked, the initials "H.B." were scrawled upon one side. It was pierced in the brim for a hat securer, but the elastic was missing. It was cracked, exceedingly dusty, and spotted in several places, although there seemed to have been some attempt to hide the discolored patches by smearing them with ink.

"I can see nothing," said I, handing it back.

"On the contrary, Watson, you can see everything. You fail, however, to reason from what you see."

"Then, pray tell me what you can infer from this hat?"

He picked it up and gazed at it in the fashion that was characteristic of him. "It is perhaps less suggestive than it might have been, and yet there are a few inferences that are very distinct, and a few others that are at least probable. That the man was highly intellectual is of course obvious, and also that he was fairly well-to-do within the last three years, although he has now fallen upon evil days. He had foresight, but has less now than formerly, pointing to a moral slip, which, when taken with the decline of his fortunes, seems to indicate some evil influence, probably drink, at work upon him. This may account also for the obvious fact that his wife has ceased to love him."

"My dear Holmes!"

"He has, however, retained some degree of self-respect," he continued. "He leads a sedentary life, goes out little, is out of shape entirely, is middle-aged, has grizzled hair that he has had cut within the last few days, and which he anoints with lime-cream. Also, by the way, it is extremely unlikely that he has gas in his house."

"You are certainly joking, Holmes."

"Not in the least. Is it possible that even now when I give you these results you are unable to see how they are attained?"

"I have no doubt that I am very stupid; but I must confess that I am unable to follow you. For example, how did you deduce that this man was intellectual?"

As an answer, Holmes clapped the hat upon his head. It settled on the bridge of his nose. "It is a question of capacity," said he. "A man with so large a brain must have something in it."

"The decline of his fortunes, then?"

"This hat is three years old. These flat brims curled at the edge came in fashion then. It is a hat of the very best quality. If this man could afford to buy so expensive a hat three years ago, and no hat since, then he has gone down in the world."

"Well, that is clear enough, certainly. But how about the foresight, and the moral decline?"

Sherlock Holmes laughed. "Here is the foresight," said he, putting his finger upon the little disc and loop of the hat-securer. "They are never sold upon hats.

If this man ordered one, it is a sign of foresight, since he went out of his way to take this precaution against the wind. But since he has broken the elastic and has not troubled to replace it, it is obvious that he has less foresight now than formerly, which is a distinct proof of a weakening nature. On the other hand, he has endeavored to conceal some of these stains upon the felt by daubing them with ink, which is a sign that he has not entirely lost his self-respect."

"Your reasoning is certainly plausible."

"The further points, that he is middle-aged, that his hair is grizzled, that it has been recently cut, and that he uses lime-cream, are all to be gathered from a close examination of the lower part of the lining. With the lens you can see a large number of hair ends, clean cut by the scissors of the barber. They all appear to be sticky, and there is a distinct odor of lime-cream. This dust, you will observe, is not the gritty, grey dust of the street, but the fluffy brown dust of the house, showing that it has been hung up indoors most of the time. The marks of moisture upon the inside are proof that the wearer perspired very freely and could hardly be in the best of training."

"But his wife – you said that she had ceased to love him."

"This hat has not been brushed for weeks. When I see you, my dear Watson, with a week's accumulation of dust upon your hat, and when your wife allows you to go out in such a state, I shall fear that you also have been unfortunate enough to lose your wife's affection."

"But he might be a bachelor."

"Nay, he was bringing home the goose as a peace-offering to his wife. Remember the card upon the bird's leg."

"You have an answer to everything. But how on earth do you deduce that the gas is not on in the house?"

"One wax stain, or even two, might come by chance; but, when I see five, I think that there can be little doubt that the individual must be brought into frequent contact with burning wax – walks upstairs at night probably with his hat in one hand and a candle in the other. He never got wax stains from a gas jet. Are you satisfied?"

"Well, it is very ingenious," said I; "but since there has been no crime committed and no harm done

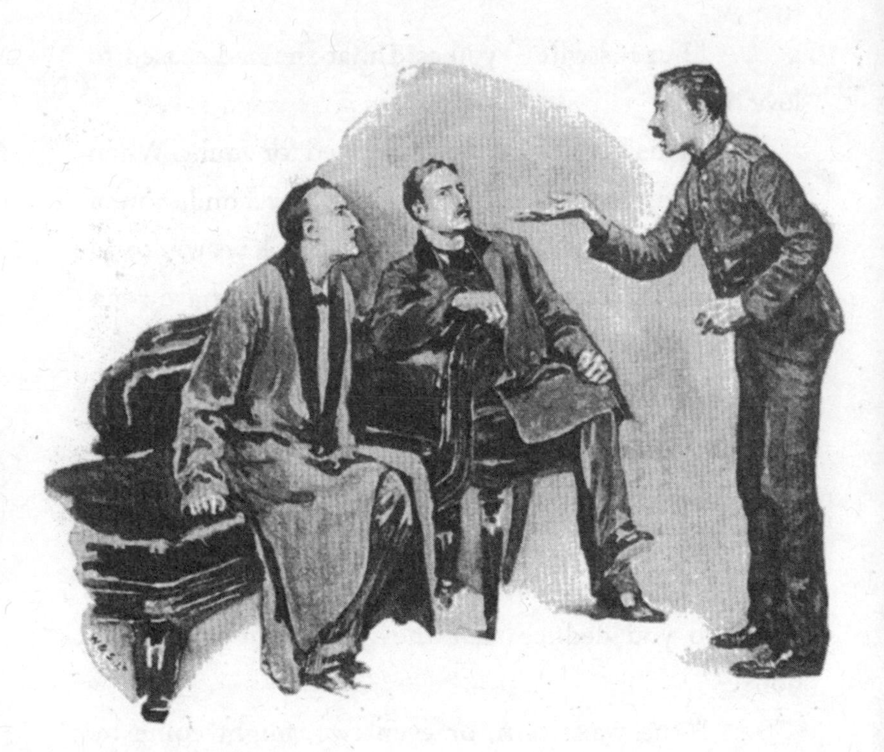

"SEE WHAT MY WIFE FOUND IN ITS THROAT."

except the loss of a goose, all this seems to be rather a waste of energy."

Sherlock Holmes had opened his mouth to reply, when the door flew open, and Peterson the commissionaire rushed in with the face of a man who is dazed with astonishment.

"The goose, Mr. Holmes! The goose, sir!" he gasped.

"Eh! What of it, then? Has it returned to life?"

"See here, sir! See what my wife found in its throat!" He held out his hand and displayed on his palm a brilliant blue stone. It was smaller than a bean in size, but of such purity and radiance that it twinkled like an electric point.

Sherlock Holmes sat up with a whistle. "By jove, Peterson," said he, "this is a treasure indeed! I suppose you know what you have got?"

"A diamond, sir! A precious stone!"

"It's more than a precious stone. It's the precious stone."

"Not the Countess of Morcar's blue carbuncle?" I blurted.

"Precisely so. I ought to know its size and shape, seeing that I have read about it in *The Times* every day lately. It is absolutely unique, and its value can only be guessed at, but the reward offered of a thousand pounds is certainly not within a twentieth part of the market price."

"A thousand pounds! Great Lord of mercy!" The commissionaire plumped down into a chair and stared from one to the other of us.

"And I have reason to know that there are sentimental considerations that would induce the Countess to part with half her fortune if she could recover the gem."

"It was lost, if I remember correctly, at the Hotel Cosmopolitan," I remarked.

"Precisely so, just five days ago. John Horner, a plumber, was accused of having taken it from the lady's jewel case. The evidence against him was so strong that the case has been referred to the Superior Court. I have some account of that matter here, I believe." He rummaged amid his newspapers, until at last he smoothed one out, doubled it over, and read the following paragraph:

HOTEL COSMOPOLITAN JEWEL ROBBERY

John Horner, 26, plumber, was brought up upon the charge of having stolen from the jewel case of the Countess of Morcar the valuable gem known as the blue carbuncle. James Ryder, upper attendant at the hotel, testified that he had shown Horner up to the dressing room of the Countess of Morcar upon the day of the robbery, in order that he might solder the grate, which was loose. He had remained with Horner a little while, but had finally been called away. On returning he found that Horner had disappeared, that the bureau had been forced open, and that the small casket in which the Countess kept her jewel was lying empty on the table. Ryder instantly gave the alarm, and Horner was arrested the same evening; but the stone could not be found. Catherine Cusack, maid to the Countess, testified to hearing Ryder's cry of dismay on discovering the robbery, and to having rushed into the room, where she found matters were as described by Ryder. Inspector Bradstreet gave evidence as to the arrest of Horner, who struggled frantically, and protested his innocence. Evidence of a previous conviction for robbery having been given against the prisoner, the magistrate refused to deal with the offense, but referred it to the Superior Court. Horner, who had shown in-

tense emotion during the proceedings, fainted away at the conclusion, and was carried out of court.

"Hum! So much for the police court," said Holmes thoughtfully, tossing aside his paper. "The question for us now to solve is the sequence of events leading from a burglarized jewel case at one end to the throat of a goose at the other. Watson, our little deductions have suddenly assumed a less innocent aspect. Here is the stone; the stone came from the goose, and the goose came from Mr. Henry Baker, the gentleman with the bad hat and all the other characteristics with which I bored you. So now we must set ourselves very seriously to finding this gentleman. To do this, we must try the simplest means first – an advertisement in all the evening papers."

"What will you say?"

"Give me a pencil and that slip of paper. Now, then: 'Found at the corner of Goodge Street, a goose and a black felt hat. Mr. Henry Baker can have them back by visiting at six-thirty this evening at 221b Baker Street.' That is clear and concise."

"Very. But will he see it?"

"Well, he is sure to keep an eye on the papers, since, to a poor man, the loss was a heavy one. He was clearly so scared by his bad luck in breaking the window, and by the approach of Peterson, that he thought of nothing but flight. But since then he must have regretted the impulse that caused him to drop his bird. Here you are, Peterson, run down to the advertising agency, and have this put in the evening papers."

"Very well, sir. And this stone?"

"Ah, yes, I shall keep the stone. Thank you. And, Peterson, buy a goose on your way back and leave it here. We must have one to give to this gentleman in place of the one your family is devouring."

When the commissionaire had gone, Holmes took up the stone and held it up against the light. "It's a fine thing," said he. "Just see how it glints and sparkles. Of course it is a focus of crime. Every good stone is. They are the devil's baits. This stone is not yet twenty years old. It was found in China, and it is remarkable in having every characteristic of the carbuncle, except that it is blue, instead of ruby red. It has already a sinister history. There have been two murders, a suicide, and several robberies brought about for the sake of this blue carbuncle.

I'll lock it up in my strongbox and drop a line to the Countess to say that we have it."

"Do you think this man Horner is innocent?"

"I cannot tell."

"Do you imagine that this other one, Henry Baker, had anything to do with the matter?"

"It is, I think, more likely that Henry Baker is an absolutely innocent man, who had no idea that the bird he was carrying was of more value than if it were made of gold. That, however, I shall determine by a very simple test, if we have an answer to our advertisement."

"And you can do nothing until then?"

"Nothing."

"In that case I shall come back in the evening, to see the solution to so tangled a business."

"Very glad to see you. I dine at seven."

It was a little after half-past six when I found myself back in Baker Street. As I approached the house I saw a tall man in a soft woolen cap, with a coat that was buttoned up to his chin, waiting outside. Just as I arrived, the door was opened, and we were shown up together to Holmes's room.

"Mr. Henry Baker, I believe," said he, rising and

greeting his visitor. "Pray take this chair by the fire, Mr. Baker. Ah, Watson, you have come at the right time. Is that your hat, Mr. Baker?"

"Yes, sir, that is undoubtedly my hat."

He was a large man, with rounded shoulders, a massive head, and a broad, intelligent face with a grizzled brown beard. His rusty black coat was buttoned up in front and his wrists protruded from his sleeves. He spoke in a choppy fashion, choosing his words, and gave the impression of a man of learning who had had a run of bad luck.

"We have kept these things some days," said Holmes, "because we expected to see an advertisement from you giving your address. I am at a loss to know now why you did not advertise."

Our visitor gave a rather shamefaced laugh. "Money has not been so plentiful with me as it once was," he remarked. "I had no doubt that the thugs who assaulted me had carried off both my hat and the bird. I did not care to spend more money in a hopeless attempt at recovering them."

"Very naturally. By the way, about the bird – we were compelled to eat it."

"To eat it!" Our visitor half rose from his chair in his excitement.

"Yes. It would have been no use to anyone had we not. But I presume that this other goose on the sideboard, which is about the same weight and fresh, will answer your purpose equally well?"

"Oh certainly, certainly!" answered Mr. Baker, with a sigh of relief.

"Of course, we still have the feathers, legs, throat, and so on of your bird, if you wish – "

The man burst into a hearty laugh. "They might be useful to me as relics of my adventure," said he, "but, no, sir, I think that, with your permission, I will confine my attentions to the excellent bird that I see upon the sideboard."

Sherlock Holmes glanced sharply across at me with a slight shrug of his shoulders.

"There is your hat, then, and there your bird," said he. "By the way, would you tell me where you got the other one from? I am a fowl fancier, and I have seldom seen a better-grown goose."

"Certainly, sir," said Baker, who had risen and tucked his newly gained property under his arm. "There

BAKER TUCKED HIS NEWLY GAINED PROPERTY UNDER HIS ARM.

are a few of us who frequent the Alpha Inn near the museum. This year our good host, Windigate by name, instituted a goose club, by which, for a few pence every week, we were to receive a bird for Christmas. My pence were duly paid, and the rest is familiar to you. I am much indebted to you, sir." He bowed solemnly to both of us and strode off upon his way.

"So much for Mr. Henry Baker," said Holmes. "It is certain that he knows nothing whatever about the matter. Are you hungry, Watson?"

"Not particularly."

"Then I suggest that we turn our dinner into a supper and follow this clue while it is still hot."

"By all means."

It was a bitter night, so we drew on our coats and wrapped scarves around our throats. In a quarter of an hour we were at the Alpha Inn. Holmes opened the door of the bar and ordered two glasses of beer from the ruddy-faced landlord.

"Your beer should be excellent, if it is as good as your geese," he said.

"My geese!" The man seemed surprised.

"Yes. I was speaking half an hour ago to Mr.

Henry Baker, a member of your goose club."

"Ah! yes, I see. But, sir, them's not our geese."

"Indeed! Whose, then?"

"Well, I get the two dozen from a salesman in Covent Garden."

"Indeed! I know some of them. Who was it?"

"Breckinridge is his name."

"Ah! I don't know him. Well, here's to your good health, landlord. Good night."

"Now for Mr. Breckinridge," he continued, buttoning up his coat as we came out into the frosty air. "Remember, Watson, that though we have so homely a thing as a goose at one end of this chain, we have at the other a man who will get seven years in jail, unless we can establish his innocence. It is possible that our inquiry may but confirm his guilt; but, in any case, we have a line of investigation that has been missed by the police, and which luck has placed in our hands. Let us follow it out to the bitter end."

We passed through a zigzag of slums to Covent Garden Market. One of the largest stalls bore the name of Breckinridge, and the proprietor was helping a boy put up the shutters.

"Good evening. It's a cold night," said Holmes.

The salesman nodded, shooting a questioning glance at my companion.

"Sold out of geese, I see," continued Holmes.

"Let you have five hundred tomorrow morning."

"That's no good."

"Well, there are some on the stall with the gas flare."

"Ah, but I was recommended to you."

"Who by?"

"The landlord of the 'Alpha.' "

"Ah, yes; I sent him a couple of dozen."

"Fine birds they were, too. Where did you get them from?"

To my surprise the question provoked a burst of anger from the salesman.

"Now then, mister," said he, "what are you driving at? Let's have it straight, now."

"It is straight enough. I should like to know who sold you the geese that you supplied to the 'Alpha.' "

"Well, then, I shan't tell you. So now!"

"Oh, it is of no importance, but I don't know why you should be so upset over such a trifle."

"Upset! You'd be as upset, maybe, if you were as pestered as I am. When I pay good money for a good item, there should be an end of the business. But it's 'Where are the geese?' and 'Who did you sell the geese to?' and 'What will you take for the geese?' One would think they were the only geese in the world, for the fuss that is made over them."

"Well, I have no connection with any other people who have been making inquiries," said Holmes. "If you won't tell us the bet is off, that is all. But I'm always ready to back my opinion on a matter of fowls, and I have a fiver on it that the bird I ate is country bred."

"Well, then, you've lost your fiver, for it's town bred," snapped the salesman.

"I don't believe you."

"D'you think you know more about fowls than I, who have handled them since I was a lad? I tell you, all those birds that went to the 'Alpha' were town bred."

"You'll never persuade me to believe that."

"Will you bet, then?"

"It's merely taking your money, for I know that I am right. But I'll bet you a sovereign, just to teach you not to be stubborn."

The salesman chuckled grimly. "Bring me the books, Bill," said he.

The small boy brought round a small thin volume and a great greasy-backed one, laying them out together beneath the hanging lamp.

"Now then, Mr. Cocksure," said the salesman. "You see this little book?"

"Well?"

"That's the list of the folk from whom I buy. D'you see? Well, then, here on this page are the country folk, and the numbers after their names are where their accounts are in the big ledger. Now, then! You see this other page in red ink? Well, that is a list of my town suppliers. Now, look at that third name. Just read it out to me."

"Mrs. Oakshott, 117 Brixton Road – 249," read Holmes.

"Quite so. Now turn that up in the ledger."

Holmes turned to the page indicated. "Here you are, 'Mrs. Oakshott, 117 Brixton Road, egg and poultry supplier.' "

"Now, then, what's the last entry?"

" 'December 22. Twenty-four geese. Sold to Mr. Windigate of the Alpha.' "

"JUST READ IT OUT TO ME."

"What have you to say now?"

Sherlock Holmes looked deeply disappointed. He drew a sovereign from his pocket and threw it down upon the slab, turning away with the air of a man whose disgust is too deep for words. A few yards off he stopped under a lamp and laughed.

"I dare say that if I had put a hundred pounds down in front of him he would not have given me such complete information as was drawn from him by the idea that he was beating me on a wager," said he. "Well, Watson, the only point that remains to be determined is whether we should go on to Mrs. Oakshott tonight, or wait until tomorrow. It is clear from what that surly fellow said that others besides ourselves are anxious about the matter, and I should – "

His remarks were suddenly cut short by a loud hubbub that broke out from the stall that we had just left. Turning round we saw a little rat-faced fellow standing under the swinging lamp, while Breckinridge the salesman was shaking his fists fiercely at the cringing figure.

"If you come pestering me any more with your silly talk I'll set the dog at you," he shouted. "You bring Mrs. Oakshott here and I'll answer her, but what have you to do with it? Did I buy the geese off you?"

"No, but one of them was mine all the same," whined the little man.

"Well, then, ask Mrs. Oakshott for it."

"She told me to ask you."

"You can ask the King of Proosia, for all I care. I've had enough. Get out!" He rushed forward, and the inquirer slipped away in the dark.

"Ha, this may save us a visit to Brixton Road," whispered Holmes. "We will see what is to be made of this fellow." My companion speedily overtook the little man and touched him on the shoulder. He sprang around, and I could see in the lamp light that all the color had been driven from his face.

"Who are you, then? What do you want?" he asked in a quavering voice.

"You will excuse me," said Holmes blandly, "but I could not help overhearing the questions that you put to the salesman just now. I think that I could be of assistance to you."

"You? Who are you? How could you know anything of the matter?"

"My name is Sherlock Holmes. It is my business to know what other people don't know."

"But you can know nothing of this?"

"Excuse me, I know everything of it. You are trying to trace some geese that were sold by Mrs. Oakshott, of Brixton Road, to a salesman named Breckinridge, by

"YOU ARE THE VERY MAN."

him in turn to Mr. Windigate, of the 'Alpha,' and by him to his club, of which Mr. Henry Baker is a member."

"Oh, sir, you are the very man whom I have longed to meet," cried the little fellow. "I can hardly explain to you how interested I am in this matter."

Sherlock Holmes hailed a passing carriage. "In that case we had better discuss it in a cosy room rather than in this marketplace," said he. "But pray tell me, before we go further, who it is that I have the pleasure of assisting."

The man hesitated. "My name is John Robinson," he answered, with a sidelong glance.

"No, the real name," said Holmes sweetly. "It is always awkward doing business with an alias."

A blush sprang to the white cheeks of the stranger. "My real name is James Ryder," said he.

"Precisely so. Head attendant at the Hotel Cosmopolitan. Step into the cab, and I shall soon tell you everything you would wish to know."

The little man stood glancing from one to the other of us with half-frightened, half-hopeful eyes. Then he stepped into the cab, and soon we were back in the sitting room at Baker Street.

"Here we are!" said Holmes cheerily, as we filed into the room. "The fire looks very seasonable in this weather. You look cold, Mr. Ryder. Pray take the basket chair. Now, then! You want to know what became of those geese?"

"Yes, sir."

"Or rather, I fancy, of that goose. It was one bird, I imagine, in which you were interested – white, with a black bar across the tail."

Ryder quivered with emotion. "Oh, sir," he cried, "can you tell me where it went to?"

"It came here. And I don't wonder that you should take an interest in it. It laid an egg after it was dead – the prettiest little blue egg that ever was seen. I have it here in my museum."

Our visitor staggered to his feet and clutched the mantelpiece with his right hand. Holmes unlocked his strong-box and held up the blue carbuncle, which shone like a star. Ryder stood glaring, uncertain whether to claim or disown it.

"The game's up, Ryder," said Holmes quietly. "Hold up, man, or you'll be in the fire! Give him an arm back into his chair, Watson. Give him a dash of brandy."

For a moment he had staggered and nearly fallen, but the brandy brought color into his cheeks, and he sat staring with frightened eyes.

"I have almost every link in my hands, and all the proofs that I could possibly need, so there is little that you need tell me. Still, that little may as well be cleared up. You had heard, Ryder, of this blue stone of the Countess of Morcar's?"

"Catherine Cusack told me of it," said he, in a crackling voice.

"I see. Her ladyship's maid. The temptation of sudden wealth so easily acquired was too much for you, as it has been for better men before you; but you were not very decent in the means you used. You knew that this man Horner, the plumber, had been in trouble before, and that suspicion would rest the more readily upon him. What did you do, then? You made some small job in the lady's room – you and your confederate Cusack – and you made sure that he should be the man sent for. Then, when he had left, you burglarized the jewel case, raised the alarm, and had this unfortunate man arrested. You then – "

Ryder threw himself down suddenly and

clutched at my companion's knees. "For God's sake, have mercy!" he shrieked. "Think of my father! Of my mother! It would break their hearts. I never went wrong before! I never will again. I swear it. I'll swear it on a Bible. Oh, don't bring it into court! For Christ's sake, don't!"

"Get back into your chair!" said Holmes sternly. "It is very well to cringe and crawl now, but you thought little enough of this poor Horner in jail for a crime of which he knew nothing."

"I will flee, Mr. Holmes. I will leave the country, sir. Then the charge against him will break down."

"Hum! We will talk about that. And now let us hear a true account of the next act. How came the stone into the goose, and how came the goose into the open market? Tell us the truth, for there lies your only hope of safety."

"I will tell you it just as it happened, sir," said Ryder. "When Horner had been arrested, it seemed to me that it would be best for me to get away with the stone at once, for I did not know if the police might search me and my room. There was no place about the hotel where it would be safe. I went out, and I made for

"'HAVE MERCY!' HE SHRIEKED."

my sister's house. She lives on Brixton Road, where she fattens fowls for the market. All the way there every man I met seemed to me to be a policeman. It was a cold night, and yet sweat was pouring down my face before I came to Brixton Road. My sister asked me what was the matter, and why I was so pale. I told her that I had been upset by the jewel robbery at the hotel. Then I went into the back yard, smoked a pipe, and wondered what to do.

"I had a friend once called Maudsley, who went bad, and has been serving time in prison. One day he talked about how thieves could get rid of what they stole. I knew that he would be true to me, for I knew one or two things about him, so I made up my mind to go right on to Kilburn, where he lived, and take him into my confidence. But how to get to him in safety? I thought of the agonies I had gone through in coming from the hotel. I might at any moment be seized and searched, and there would be the stone in my coat pocket. I was leaning against the wall, looking at the geese waddling about my feet, and suddenly an idea came into my head that showed me how I could beat the best detective that ever lived.

"My sister had told me some weeks before that I might have the pick of her geese for a Christmas present, and I knew that she was always as good as her word. I would take my goose now, and in it I would carry my stone to Kilburn. There was a little shed in the yard, and behind this I drove one of the birds, a fine big one, white, with a barred tail. I caught it and, forcing its bill open, I thrust the stone down its throat as far as my finger could reach. But the creature flapped and struggled, and out came my sister to know what was the matter. As I turned to speak to her, the brute broke loose and fluttered off among the others.

" 'Whatever were you doing with that bird, Jem?' says she.

" 'Well,' said I, 'you said you'd give me one for Christmas, and I was feeling which was fattest.'

" 'Oh,' says she, 'we've set yours aside for you. It's the big, white one over yonder. There's twenty-six of them, which makes one for you, and one for us, and two dozen for the market.'

" 'Thank you, Maggie,' says I 'but if it is all the same to you I'd rather have that one I was handling just now.'

" 'The other is three pounds heavier,' she said, 'and we fattened it expressly for you.'

" 'Never mind. I'll have the other, and I'll take it now,' said I.

" 'Oh, just as you like,' said she, a little huffed. 'Which is it you want, then?'

" 'That white one, with the barred tail, right in the middle of the flock.'

" 'Oh, very well. Kill it and take it with you.'

"Well, I did what she said, Mr. Holmes, and I carried the bird all the way to Kilburn. I told my pal what I had done. He laughed until he choked, and we got a knife and opened the goose. My heart turned to water, for there was no sign of the stone, and I knew that some terrible mistake had occurred. I left the bird, rushed back to my sister's, and hurried into the back yard. There was not a bird to be seen there.

" 'Where are they all, Maggie?' I cried.

" 'Gone to Breckinridge of Covent Garden.'

" 'But was there another with a barred tail?' I asked, 'the same as the one I chose?'

" 'Yes, Jem, there were two barred-tailed ones, and I could never tell them apart.'

"Well, then, of course, I saw it all, and I ran off as hard as my feet would carry me to this man Breckinridge;

but he had sold the lot all at once, and not one word would he tell me as to where they had gone. My sister thinks that I am going mad. Sometimes I think that I am myself. And now – and now I am myself a branded thief, without ever having touched the wealth for which I sold my character. God help me! God help me!" He burst into compulsive sobbing.

There was a long silence, broken only by his heavy breathing, and by the measured tapping of Sherlock Holmes's fingertips upon the table. Then my friend rose and threw open the door.

"Get out!" said he.

"What, sir! Oh, heaven bless you!"

"No more words. Get out!"

And no more words were needed. There was a rush, a clatter upon the stairs, the bang of a door, and the rattle of running footsteps from the street.

"After all, Watson," said Holmes, reaching for his pipe, "I am not retained by the police to supply their deficiencies. If Horner were in danger it would be another thing, but this fellow will not appear against him, and the case must collapse. I suppose that I am covering up a felony, but it is just possible that I am saving a soul. This fellow will not go wrong again. He is too terribly frightened. Send him to jail now, and you make him a jailbird for life. Besides, it is the season of forgiveness. Chance has put in our way a most singular and whimsical problem, and its solution is its own reward."

The Adventure of the Copper Beeches

~❖~

IT WAS A COLD MORNING OF THE EARLY SPRING, and Sherlock Holmes and I sat after breakfast on either side of a cheery fire in Baker Street. Holmes had been silent all morning, dipping into the advertisement columns of several newspapers, until at last, giving up his search, he emerged in an ill temper.

"Watson, I fear the days of the great cases are past. Man, or at least criminal man, has lost all enterprise and originality. My own practice seems to be degenerating into an agency for recovering lost pencils and giving advice to young ladies from boarding-schools. I think that I have touched bottom at last, how-

HOLMES HAD BEEN SILENT ALL MORNING.

ever. This note I had this morning marks my zero point, I fancy. Read it!" He tossed a crumpled letter across to me.

It was dated from Montague Place upon the preceding evening, and ran thus:

Dear Mr. Holmes,

I am very anxious to consult you as to whether I should or should not accept a situation that has been offered to me as governess. I shall call at half-past ten tomorrow, if I do not inconvenience you.

Yours faithfully,
Violet Hunter

"Do you know the young lady?" I asked.

"Not I."

"It is half-past ten now."

"Yes, and no doubt that is her ring."

"It may turn out to be of more interest than you think. You remember that the affair of the blue carbuncle, which appeared to be a mere whim at first, developed into a serious investigation. It may be so in this case also."

"Well, let us hope so! But our doubts will very soon be solved, for here, unless I am much mistaken, is the person in question."

As he spoke the door opened, and a young lady entered the room. She was plainly but neatly dressed, with a bright, quick face, freckled, and with the brisk manner of a woman who has had to make her own way in the world.

"You will excuse my troubling you, I am sure," said she, as my companion rose to greet her, "but I have had a very strange experience, and as I have no relations from whom I could ask advice, I thought that perhaps you would be kind enough to tell me what I should do."

"Pray take a seat, Miss Hunter. I shall be happy to do anything that I can to serve you."

I could see that Holmes was favorably impressed by the manner of his new client. He looked her over, in his searching fashion, and then composed himself to listen to her story.

"I have been a governess for five years," said she, "in the family of Colonel Spence Munro. Two months ago the Colonel received an appointment in Nova Scotia and took his children over to America with him, so that I found myself without a situation. I advertised, but without success. At last the little money that I had saved began to run short, and I was at my wits' end as to what I should do.

"There is a well-known agency for governesses called Westaway's, and there I used to call about once a week to see whether anything had turned up that might suit me. Westaway was the name of the founder of the business, but it is really managed by Miss Stoper. She sits in her own little office, and the ladies who seek employment wait in an outside room, to be shown in one by one. She consults her ledgers to see whether she has anything that would suit them.

"Well, when I called last week I was shown into the little office as usual, but Miss Stoper was not alone. A very stout man with a smiling face, and a heavy chin, sat at her elbow with a pair of glasses on his nose, looking very earnestly at the ladies who entered. As I came in he gave a jump in his chair and turned quickly to Miss Stoper:

" 'That will do,' said he; 'I could not ask for anything better. Capital!' He seemed enthusiastic and rubbed his hands together in a genial fashion.

" 'You are looking for a situation as governess, miss?' he asked.

" 'Yes, sir.'

" 'And what salary do you ask?'

THAT WILL DO.

" 'I had four pounds a month in my last place with Colonel Spence Munro.'

" 'Oh, tut, tut!' he cried, throwing his fat hands out into the air. 'How could anyone offer so pitiful a sum to a lady with such attractions and accomplishments?'

" 'My accomplishments, sir, may be less than you imagine,' said I.

" 'Tut, tut!' he cried. 'This is all quite beside the question. The point is, have you or have you not the bearing and deportment of a lady? There it is in a nutshell. If you have not, you are not fitted for the rearing of a child who may some day play a considerable part in the history of the country. But if you have, why, then how could any gentleman ask you to accept anything under three figures? Your salary with me, madam, would begin at a hundred pounds a year.'

"You may imagine, Mr. Holmes, that to me, destitute as I was, such an offer seemed almost too good to be true. The gentleman, however, seeing perhaps the look of disbelief upon my face, opened a wallet and took out a note.

" 'It is also my custom,' said he, smiling, 'to advance to my young ladies half their salary beforehand, so that they may meet any little expenses of their journey and their wardrobe.'

"It seemed to me that I had never met so thoughtful a man. As I was already in debt, the advance was a great convenience, and yet there was something unnatural about the whole transaction that made me wish to know a little more before I quite committed myself.

" 'May I ask where you live, sir?' said I.

" 'Hampshire. Charming rural place. The Copper Beeches, five miles on the far side of Winchester. It is the most lovely country, my dear young lady, and the dearest old country house.'

" 'And my duties, sir? I should be glad to know what they would be.'

" 'One child – one dear little romper just six years old. Oh, if you could see him killing cockroaches with a slipper! Smack! smack! smack! Three gone before you could wink!' He leaned back in his chair and laughed again.

"I was a little startled at the nature of the child's amusement, but the father's laughter made me think that perhaps he was joking.

" 'My sole duties, then,' I asked, 'are to take charge of a single child?'

" 'No, no, not the sole, my dear young lady,' he cried. 'Your duty would be to obey any little commands that my wife might give, provided always that they were such as a lady might with propriety obey. You see no difficulty, heh?'

" 'I should be happy to make myself useful.'

" 'Quite so. In dress now, for example! We are faddy people, you know – faddy, but kindhearted. If you were asked to wear any dress that we might give you, you would not object to our little whim. Heh?'

" 'No,' said I, astonished at his words.

" 'Or to sit here, or sit there, that would not be offensive, to you?'

" 'Oh, no.'

" 'Or to cut your hair quite short before you come to us?'

"I could hardly believe my ears. As you may observe, Mr. Holmes, my hair is luxuriant, and of a peculiar tint of chestnut. I could not dream of sacrificing it in this off-hand fashion.

" 'I am afraid that that is quite impossible,' said I. He had been watching me eagerly, and I could see a shadow pass over his face as I spoke.

" 'I am afraid that is quite essential,' said he. 'It is a little fancy of my wife's, and ladies' fancies, you know, madam, must be consulted. And so you won't cut your hair?'

" 'No, sir, I really could not,' I answered firmly.

" 'Ah, very well; then that settles the matter. It is

a pity, because in other respects you would have done very nicely. In that case, Miss Stoper, I had best inspect a few more of your ladies.'

"Miss Stoper had sat all this while busy with her papers, but she glanced at me now with such annoyance on her face that I could not help suspecting that she had lost a handsome commission through my refusal.

" 'Do you desire your name to be kept upon the books?' she asked.

" 'If you please, Miss Stoper.'

" 'Well, really, it seems rather useless, since you refuse the most excellent offers,' said she sharply. 'You can hardly expect us to exert ourselves to find another such opening for you.' She struck a gong, and I was shown out.

"Well, Mr. Holmes, when I got back to my lodging and found little in the cupboard, and two or three bills upon the table, I began to ask myself whether I had not done a very foolish thing. Few governesses in England get a hundred a year. Besides, what use was my hair to me? Next day I was inclined to think that I had made a mistake, and by the day after I was sure of it. I had almost overcome my pride, so far as to go back to the agency and inquire whether the place was still open, when I received this letter from the gentleman himself. I have it here, and I will read it to you:

The Copper Beeches,
Near Winchester

Dear Miss Hunter,

Miss Stoper has kindly given me your address, and I write to ask whether you have reconsidered your decision. My wife is anxious that you should come, for she has been much attracted by my description of you. We are willing to give thirty pounds a quarter, or £120 a year, to recompense you for any inconvenience our fads may cause you. They are not very exacting after all. My wife is fond of a particular shade of electric blue and would like you to wear such a dress indoors in the morning. You need not go to the expense of purchasing one, as we have one belonging to my dear daughter Alice (now in Philadelphia) which would, I think, fit you very well. Then, as to sitting here or there, or amusing yourself in any manner indicated, that need cause you no inconvenience. As regards your hair, it is no doubt a pity, especially as I could not help noticing its beauty during our interview, but I am afraid that I must remain firm upon this point. I only hope that the increased salary may recompense you for the loss. Your duties, as far as the child is concerned, are very light. Now do try to come, and I shall meet you with the cart at Winchester. Let me know your train.

Yours faithfully,

Jephro Rucastle

"That is the letter, Mr. Holmes, and my mind is made up that I will accept it. However, before taking the final step, I should like to submit the matter to your consideration."

"Well, Miss Hunter, if your mind is made up, that settles the question," said Holmes, smiling.

"But you would not advise me to refuse?"

"I confess that it is not the situation that I should like to see a sister of mine apply for."

"What is the meaning of it all, Mr. Holmes?"

"Ah, I have no facts. I cannot tell. Perhaps you have yourself formed some opinion?"

"Well, there seems to me to be only one solution. Mr. Rucastle seemed to be a very kind, good-natured man. Is it not possible that his wife is a lunatic, that he desires to keep the matter quiet for fear she should be taken to an asylum, and that he humors her fancies in order to prevent an outbreak."

"That is a possible solution – as matters stand, it is the most probable one. But in any case it does not seem to be a nice household for a young lady."

"But the money, Mr. Holmes, the money!"

"Yes, the pay is good – too good. That is what makes me uneasy. Why should they give £120 a year, when they could have their pick for £40?"

"I thought that if I told you the circumstances, you would understand afterwards if I wanted your help. I should feel so much stronger if I felt that you were behind me."

"Oh, you may carry that feeling away with you.

HOLMES SHOOK HIS HEAD GRAVELY.

Your problem promises to be the most interesting that has come my way for some months. There is something distinctly unusual about some of the features. If you find yourself in danger –"

"Danger! What danger do you foresee?"

Holmes shook his head gravely. "It would cease to be a danger if we could define it," said he. "But at any time, day or night, a telegram would bring me down to your help."

"That is enough." She rose briskly from her chair, with the anxiety swept from her face. "I shall go to Hampshire easy in my mind. I shall write to Mr. Rucastle at once, sacrifice my hair tonight, and start for Winchester tomorrow." With a few grateful words to Holmes she bade us goodnight.

"At least," said I, "she seems to be a young lady who is able to take care of herself."

"And she would need to be," said Holmes gravely. "I am much mistaken if we do not hear from her before many days are past."

It was not very long before my friend's prediction was fulfilled. Two weeks went by, during which I frequently wondered what strange situation this lonely woman had strayed into. The unusual salary, the curious conditions, the light duties, all pointed to something abnormal. As to Holmes, I observed that he sat frequently for half an hour on end, with knitted brows, but he swept the matter away with a wave of his hand when I mentioned it. "Facts! facts! facts!" he cried impatiently. "I can't make bricks without clay."

The telegram we eventually received came late one night, just as I was thinking of turning in, and Holmes was settling down to one of those all-night researches that he frequently indulged in. He opened the yellow envelope and then, glancing at the message, threw it across to me.

"Just look up the trains," said he, and turned back to his studies.

The summons was a brief and urgent one.

Please be at the Black Swan Hotel at Winchester at midday tomorrow. Do come! I am at my wits' end.

Hunter

By eleven o'clock the next day we were well upon our way. Holmes had been buried in the morning newspapers, but after we had passed the Hampshire border he threw them down and began to admire the scenery.

"Well, Watson, it is clear that Miss Hunter is not personally threatened."

"I AM SO DELIGHTED THAT YOU HAVE COME."

"No. If she can come to Winchester to meet us, she can get away."

"Quite so. She has her freedom."

"What can be the matter, then? Can you suggest no explanation?"

"I have devised seven separate explanations, each of which would cover the facts as far as we know them. But which of these is correct can be determined only by the fresh information that we shall no doubt find waiting for us."

The "Black Swan" is an inn of repute close to the station, and there we found the young lady waiting for us. She had engaged a sitting room, and our lunch awaited us upon the table.

"I am so delighted that you have come," she said earnestly. "Your advice will be altogether invaluable to me."

"Pray tell us what has happened to you."

"I will do so, and I must be quick, for I have promised Mr. Rucastle to be back before three. I got his permission to come into town this morning, though he didn't know the purpose."

"Let us have everything in its due order." Holmes thrust his long thin legs out towards the fire and composed himself to listen.

"In the first place, I have met with no actual ill

treatment from Mr. and Mrs. Rucastle. It is only fair to say that. But I cannot understand their reasons for their conduct. But you shall have it all just as it occurred. When I came down, Mr. Rucastle met me here and drove me in his cart to Copper Beeches. It is, as he said, beautifully situated, but it is not beautiful in itself. It is a large square block of a house all stained and streaked with damp weather. There are woods on three sides, and on the fourth a field slopes down to the high road. A clump of copper beeches in front of the hall door has given its name to the place.

"I was driven over by my employer, who was as amiable as ever, and was introduced that evening to his wife and the child. There was no truth, Mr. Holmes, in our conjecture. Mrs. Rucastle is not mad. I found her to be a silent, pale-faced woman, much younger than her husband, not more than thirty, I think, while he can hardly be less than forty-five. I have gathered that they have been married about seven years, that he was a widower, and that his only child by his first wife was the daughter who has gone to Philadelphia. Mr. Rucastle told me in private that the reason she left them was that she had an unreasonable aversion to her stepmother. As the daughter could not have been less than twenty, I can imagine that her position must have been uncomfortable with her father's young wife.

"Mrs. Rucastle seemed to me to be colorless in mind as well as in feature. She impressed me neither favorably nor the reverse. It was easy to see that she was passionately devoted both to her husband and to her little son. He was kind to her also in his boisterous fashion, and on the whole they seemed to be a happy couple. And yet she had some secret sorrow, this woman. She would often be lost deep in thought, with the saddest look on her face. More than once I found her in tears. I thought sometimes that it was her child that weighed upon her mind, for I have never met so utterly spoilt and so ill-natured a creature. His whole life appears to be spent in savage fits of passion and gloomy intervals of sulking. Giving pain to any creature weaker than himself seems to be his one idea of amusement. But I would rather not talk about the child, Mr. Holmes. Indeed, he has little to do with my story."

"I am glad of all details," remarked my friend, "whether they seem to you to be relevant or not."

"I shall try not to miss anything of importance.

One unpleasant thing about the house, which struck me at once, was the appearance and conduct of the servants. There are only two, a man and his wife. Toller, for that's his name, is a rough, uncouth man, with grizzled hair and whiskers, and a perpetual smell of drink. Twice since I have been with them he has been drunk, and yet Mr. Rucastle seemed to take no notice of it. Toller's wife is a tall and strong woman with a sour face, as silent as Mrs. Rucastle, and much less amiable. They are a most unpleasant couple, but fortunately I spend most of my time in the nursery and my own room, which are next to each other in one corner of the building.

"For two days after my arrival, my life was quiet; on the third, Mrs. Rucastle came down after breakfast and whispered something to her husband.

" 'Oh yes,' said he, turning to me, 'we are very much obliged to you, Miss Hunter, for falling in with our whims so far as to cut your hair. We shall now see how the electric blue dress will become you. You will find it laid upon the bed in your room, and if you would put it on, we should both be extremely obliged.'

"The dress I found waiting for me was of a peculiar shade of blue. It was of excellent material, but it bore unmistakable signs of having been worn before. It could not have been a better fit if I had been measured for it. Both Mr. and Mrs. Rucastle expressed delight at the look of it. They were waiting for me in the drawing room. A chair had been placed close to the central window, with its back turned towards it. I was asked to sit, and then Mr. Rucastle, walking up and down on the other side of the room, began to tell me the funniest stories that I have ever listened to. I laughed until I was quite weary. Mrs. Rucastle, however, never so much as smiled, but sat with her hands in her lap, and a sad, anxious look upon her face. After an hour or so, Mr. Rucastle remarked that it was time to begin the duties of the day, and that I might change my dress and go to little Edward in the nursery.

"Two days later this same performance was gone through under exactly similar circumstances. Again I changed my dress, again I sat in the window, and again I laughed heartily at the funny stories of which my employer had an immense collection, and which he told most skillfully. Then he handed me a novel, and, moving my chair a little sideways, begged me to read aloud to him. I read for about ten minutes; then he ordered me to cease and change my dress.

"I READ FOR ABOUT TEN MINUTES."

"You can easily imagine, Mr. Holmes, how curious I became as to what the meaning of this performance could possibly be. They were always careful to turn my face away from the window, so that I became consumed with the desire to see what was going on behind my back. At first it seemed impossible, but I soon devised a means. My hand mirror had been broken, so I concealed a little of the glass in my handkerchief. On the next occasion, in the midst of my laughter, I put my handkerchief up to my eyes and was able to see all there was behind me. There was nothing.

"At least, that was my first impression. At the second glance, however, I saw a man standing in the road, a small bearded man in a grey suit, who seemed to be looking in my direction. The road is an important highway, and there are usually people there. This man, however, was leaning against the railings that bordered our field and was looking earnestly. I lowered my handkerchief and glanced at Mrs. Rucastle, to find her eyes fixed upon me with a searching gaze. I am convinced that she had discovered that I had a mirror and had seen what was behind me. She rose at once.

" 'Jephro,' said she, 'there is a fellow upon the road who stares up at Miss Hunter.'

" 'No friend of yours, Miss Hunter?' he asked.

" 'No; I know no one in these parts.'

" 'Dear me! How very impertinent! Kindly turn round and motion him to go away.'

" 'Surely it would be better to take no notice?'

" 'No, no, we should have him loitering here always. Kindly turn round and wave him away.'

"I did as I was told, and Mrs. Rucastle drew down the blind. That was a week ago, and from that time I have not sat in the window, nor worn the blue dress, nor seen the man in the road."

"Pray continue your tale," said Holmes.

"You will find it rather disconnected, I fear, and there may be little relation between the different incidents of which I speak. On the very first day that I was at Copper Beeches, Mr. Rucastle took me to a small outbuilding near the kitchen door. As we approached it, I heard the rattling of a chain and the sound of a large animal moving.

" 'Look in here!' said Mr. Rucastle, showing me a slit between two planks. 'Is he not a beauty?'

"I looked through, conscious of two glowing eyes and a figure huddled in darkness.

" 'Don't be frightened,' said my employer, laughing at the start that I had given. 'It's only Carlo, my mastiff. I call him mine, but really old Toller is the only man who can do anything with him. We feed him once a day, and not too much then, so that he is always keen. Toller lets him loose every night. God help the trespasser whom he lays his fangs upon. For goodness' sake don't ever set your foot over the threshold at night.'

"The warning was no idle one, for two nights later I happened to look out of my bedroom window. It was a beautiful moonlight night, and the lawn in front of the house was almost as bright as day. I was rapt in the peaceful beauty of the scene, when I was aware that something was moving under the shadow of the copper beeches. As it emerged into the moonshine I saw it was a giant dog, as large as a calf, with hanging jowl, black muzzle, and huge bones. It walked slowly across the lawn and vanished into the shadows. That dreadful sight sent a chill to my heart, which I do not think any burglar could have done.

"And now I have a very strange experience to tell

you. I had, as you know, cut off my hair in London, and I had placed it in a great coil at the bottom of my trunk. One evening, after the child was in bed, I began examining the furniture of my room and rearranging my own little things. There was an old chest of drawers in the room, the two upper ones empty and open, the lower one locked. I had filled the two with my linen, and as I still had much to pack away, I was naturally annoyed at not having the use of the third drawer. It struck me that it might have been fastened by mistake, so I took out my bunch of keys and tried to open it. The very first key fit to perfection, and I drew the drawer open. There was only one thing in it, but I am sure that you would never guess what it was. It was my coil of hair.

"I took it up and examined it. It was of the same peculiar tint and the same thickness. But then the impossibility of the thing occurred to me. How could my hair have been locked in the drawer? With trembling hands I undid my trunk and drew from the bottom my own hair. I laid the two tresses together, and I assure you they were identical. Was it not extraordinary? Puzzle as I would, I could make nothing at all of what it meant. I returned the strange hair to the drawer, and I said noth-

"I TOOK IT UP AND EXAMINED IT."

ing of the matter to the Rucastles, as I felt that I had put myself in the wrong by opening a drawer that they had locked.

"I am naturally observant, Mr. Holmes, and I soon had a pretty good plan of the whole house in my head. There was one wing, however, that appeared not to be inhabited. A door opposite to that which led into the quarters of the Tollers opened into this suite, but it was always locked. One day, however, as I ascended the stair, I met Mr. Rucastle coming out this door, his keys in his hand, and a look on his face that made him a very different person from the jovial man to whom I was accustomed. His cheeks were red, his brow was all crinkled with anger, and the veins stood out at his temples. He locked the door and hurried past me without a word or a look.

"This aroused my curiosity, so when I went out for a walk in the grounds with the child, I strolled round to see the windows of this part of the house. There were four, three of which were simply dirty. The fourth was shuttered up. They were evidently all deserted. As I strolled up and down, glancing at them occasionally, Mr. Rucastle came out to me, as merry and jovial as ever.

" 'Ah!' said he, 'you must not think me rude if I passed you without a word, my dear young lady. I was preoccupied with business matters.'

"I assured him that I was not offended. 'By the way,' said I, 'you seem to have quite a suite of spare rooms up there, and one of them has the shutters up.'

" 'Photography is one of my hobbies,' said he. 'I have made my darkroom up there. But, dear me! what an observant young lady we have come upon.' He spoke in a jesting tone, but there was no jest in his eyes as he looked at me. I read suspicion there, and annoyance, but no jest.

"Well, Mr. Holmes, from the moment that I understood that there was something about that suite of rooms that I was not to know, I was all on fire to go over them. It was not mere curiosity. It was more a feeling of duty – a feeling that some good might come from my penetrating to this place. They talk of woman's instinct; perhaps it was woman's instinct that gave me that feeling. At any rate, I was keenly on the lookout for any chance to pass the forbidden door.

"Yesterday the chance came. Besides Mr. Rucastle, both Toller and his wife find something to do in these deserted rooms. I once saw him carry a large black linen bag through the door. Recently he has been drinking hard, and yesterday evening he was very drunk.

When I came upstairs, there was the key in the door. Mr. and Mrs. Rucastle were both downstairs, and the child was with them, so that I had an admirable opportunity. I turned the key gently, opened the door, and slipped through.

"There was a little passage in front of me, which turned at a right angle at the farther end. Round this corner were three doors in a line, the first and third of which were open. They each led into an empty room, dusty and cheerless. The center door was closed, and across it had been fastened one of the broad bars of an iron bed, padlocked at one end to a ring in the wall, and fastened at the other with heavy cord. The door itself was locked as well. This barricaded door corresponded clearly with the shuttered window outside. I could see by the glimmer from beneath it that the room was not in darkness. Evidently a skylight let in light from above. As I stood in the passage gazing at this sinister door, I suddenly heard the sound of steps within the room and saw a shadow pass back and forth against the slit of dim light that shone out from under the door. A mad, unreasoning terror rose up in me at the sight, Mr. Holmes. My nerves failed me, and I turned and ran. I rushed down the passage, through the door, and straight into the arms of Mr. Rucastle, who was waiting outside.

" 'So,' said he, smiling, 'it was you, then. I thought it must be when I saw the door open.'

" 'Oh, I am so frightened!' I panted.

" 'My dear young lady! my dear young lady!' – how caressing and soothing his manner was – 'what has frightened you, my dear young lady?'

"But his voice was just a little too coaxing. He overdid it. I was keenly on my guard against him.

" 'I was foolish enough to go into the empty wing,' I answered. 'But it is so lonely and eerie that I was frightened. It is so dreadfully still there!'

" 'Only that?' said he, looking at me keenly.

" 'Why, what do you think?' I asked.

" 'Why do you think that I lock this door?'

" 'I am sure that I do not know.'

" 'It is to keep people out who have no business there. Do you see?' He was still smiling in the most amiable manner.

" 'I am sure if I had known – '

" 'Well, then, you know now. And if you put your foot over that threshold again' – instantly the smile

"'OH! I AM SO FRIGHTENED!' I PANTED."

hardened into a grin of rage, and he glared down at me, 'I'll throw you to the mastiff.'

"I was so terrified that I rushed past him into my room. I remember nothing until I found myself lying on my bed trembling all over. Then I thought of you, Mr. Holmes. I could not live there longer without some advice. I was frightened of the house, of the man, of the woman, of the servants, even of the child. They were all horrible to me. Of course I might have fled, but my curiosity was almost as strong as my fears. My mind was soon made up. I would send you a wire. I put on my hat and cloak, went down to the office, which is about half a mile from the house, and then returned, feeling very much easier. I slipped back into the house in safety and lay awake half the night in my joy at the thought of seeing you. I had no difficulty in getting leave to come to Winchester this morning, but I must be back before three o'clock. Mr. and Mrs. Rucastle are going on a visit and will be away all the evening, so that I must look after the child. I have told you all my adventures, Mr. Holmes, and I should be very glad if you could tell me what it all means, and, above all, what I should do."

Holmes and I had listened spellbound to this extraordinary story. My friend rose now and paced up and down the room, his hands in his pockets and a grave expression upon his face.

"Is Toller still drunk?" he asked.

"Yes. I heard his wife tell Mrs. Rucastle that she could do nothing with him."

"And the Rucastles go out tonight?"

"Yes."

"Is there a cellar with a good strong lock?"

"Yes, the wine cellar."

"You seem to me to have acted all through this matter like a brave and sensible girl, Miss Hunter. Do you think that you could perform one more feat?"

"I will try. What is it?"

"We shall be at the Copper Beeches by seven o'clock. The Rucastles will be gone by that time, and Toller will, we hope, be incapable. There remains only Mrs. Toller, who might give the alarm. If you could send her into the cellar, on some errand, and then turn the key upon her, you would facilitate matters immensely."

"I will do it."

"Excellent! We shall then look thoroughly into

the affair. Of course there is only one possible explanation. You have been brought here to impersonate someone, and the real person is imprisoned in this chamber. That is obvious. As to who the prisoner is, I have no doubt that it is the daughter, Miss Alice Rucastle, who was said to have gone to America. You were chosen because you closely resemble her in height, figure, and the color of your hair. Hers had been cut off, very possibly in some illness, and so, of course, yours had to be sacrificed also. The man in the road was, undoubtedly, some friend of hers – possibly her fiancé. No doubt as you wore the girl's dress and were so like her, he was convinced from your laughter that Miss Rucastle was perfectly happy and no longer desired his attentions. The dog is let loose at night to prevent him from communicating with her. So much is clear. The most serious point in the case is the disposition of the child."

"What on earth has that to do with it?" I asked.

"My dear Watson, I frequently gain my first insight into the character of parents by studying their children. This child is abnormally cruel. Whether he derives this from his smiling father, as I suspect, or from his mother, it bodes evil for the poor girl who is in their power."

"I am sure that you are right, Mr. Holmes," cried our client. "A thousand things come back to me that make me certain. Oh, let us lose not an instant in bringing help to this poor creature."

"We must be careful, for we are dealing with a cunning man. We can do nothing until seven o'clock. At that hour we shall be with you, and it will not be long before we solve the mystery."

We were as good as our word, for it was just seven when we reached the Copper Beeches. Miss Hunter was standing smiling on the doorstep.

"Have you managed it?" asked Holmes.

A loud thudding noise came from somewhere downstairs. "That is Mrs. Toller in the cellar," said she. "Her husband lies snoring on the kitchen rug. Here are his keys."

"You have done well indeed!" cried Holmes, with enthusiasm. "Now lead the way, and we shall soon see the end of this sinister business."

We passed up the stair, unlocked the door, followed on down a passage, and found ourselves in front of the barricade that Miss Hunter had described. Holmes cut the cord and removed the bar. Then he tried the various keys in the lock, but without success. No sound came from within, and at the silence Holmes's face clouded over.

"I hope that we are not too late," said he. "I think, Miss Hunter, that we had better go in without you. Now, Watson, put your shoulder to it, and we shall see whether we cannot make our way in."

It was an old rickety door and gave at once before our united strength. Together we rushed into the room. It was empty. There was no furniture except a little bed, a small table, and a basketful of linen. The skylight above was open, and the prisoner gone.

"There has been some villainy here," said Holmes. "Rucastle has guessed Miss Hunter's intentions and has carried his victim off."

"But how?"

"Through the skylight. We shall soon see how he managed it." He swung himself up, onto the roof. "Ah, yes," he cried, "here's the end of a long ladder against the eaves. That is how he did it."

"But it is impossible," said Miss Hunter. "The ladder was not there when the Rucastles went away."

"He has come back and done it. I tell you that he

"VILLAIN!" SAID HE, "WHERE IS YOUR DAUGHTER?"

is a clever and dangerous man. I should not be very much surprised if this were he whose step I hear now upon the stair. Watson, have your pistol ready."

The words were hardly out of his mouth before a man appeared at the door of the room, a very fat and burly man, with a heavy stick in his hand. Miss Hunter screamed and shrunk against the wall at the sight of him, but Sherlock Holmes sprang forward and confronted him.

"Villain," said he, "where's your daughter?"

The fat man cast his eyes round, and then up at the open skylight.

"It is for me to ask you that," he shrieked, "you thieves! Spies and thieves! I have caught you, have I? You are in my power. I'll serve you!" He turned and clattered down the stairs.

"He's gone for the dog!" cried Miss Hunter.

"I have my revolver," said I.

"Better close the front door," cried Holmes, and we all rushed down the stairs together. We had hardly reached the hall when we heard the baying of a hound, and then a scream of agony. An elderly man with a red face and shaking limbs came staggering out a side door.

"My God!" he cried. "Someone has loosed the dog. It's not been fed for two days. Quick, quick, or it'll be too late!"

Holmes and I rushed out and round the house, with Toller hurrying behind us. There was the huge famished brute, its black muzzle buried in Rucastle's throat, while he writhed and screamed upon the ground.

"RUNNING UP, I BLEW ITS BRAINS OUT."

Running up, I blew its brains out, and it fell over with its keen white teeth still meeting in the great creases of Rucastle's neck. With much labor we separated them and carried him, living but horribly mangled, into the house. We laid him upon the drawing room sofa and dispatched the sobered Toller to bear the news to his wife. I did what I could to relieve his pain. We were all assembled round him when the door opened, and a tall, gaunt woman entered the room.

"Mrs. Toller!" cried Miss Hunter.

"Yes, miss. Mr. Rucastle let me out when he came back, before he went up to you. Ah, miss, it is a pity you didn't let me know what you were planning, for I would have told you that your pains were wasted."

"Ha!" said Holmes, looking keenly at her. "It is clear that Mrs. Toller knows more about this matter than anyone else."

"Yes, sir, I do, and I am ready enough to tell what I know."

"Then pray sit down, and let us hear it, for there are several points on which I must confess that I am still in the dark."

"I will soon make it clear to you," said she, "and I'd have done so before now if I could have got out from the cellar. If there's police court business over this, you'll remember that I was the one that stood your friend, and that I was Miss Alice's friend too.

"She was never happy at home, Miss Alice wasn't, from the time that her father married again. She had no say in anything but it never really became bad for her until after she met Mr. Fowler at a friend's house. As well as I could learn, Miss Alice had rights of her own by will, but she was so quiet and patient that she never said a word about them, but just left everything in Mr. Rucastle's hands. He knew he was safe with her, but when there was a chance of a husband coming forward, who would ask for all that the law could give him, then her father thought it time to put a stop to it. He wanted her to sign a paper so that whether she married or not, he could use her money. When she wouldn't do it, he kept on worrying her until she got brain fever, and for six weeks was at death's door. Then she got better at last, all worn to a shadow, and with her beautiful hair cut off; but that didn't make no change in her young man, and he stuck to her as true as man could be."

"Ah," said Holmes, "I can deduce all that remains. Mr. Rucastle, then, I presume, took to this system of imprisonment?"

"Yes, sir."

"And brought Miss Hunter down from London in order to get rid of the disagreeable persistence of Mr. Fowler."

"That was it, sir."

"But Mr. Fowler, being a persevering man, succeeded by **certain arguments, metallic and otherwise,** in convincing you that your interests were the same as his."

CERTAIN ARGUMENTS, METALLIC AND OTHERWISE Money.

"Mr. Fowler was a kind-spoken, free-handed gentleman," said Mrs. Toller serenely.

"And in this way he managed that your good man should have plenty to drink, and that a ladder should be ready at the moment when your master had gone out."

"You have it, sir, just as it happened."

"I am sure that we owe you an apology, Mrs. Toller," said Holmes, "for you have certainly cleared up everything that puzzled us. And here comes the country surgeon and Mrs. Rucastle, so I think, Watson, that we had best escort Miss Hunter back to Winchester."

And thus was solved the mystery of the sinister house with the copper beeches in front. Mr. Rucastle survived, but was always a broken man, kept alive solely through the care of his devoted wife. They still live with their old servants. Mr. Fowler and Miss Rucastle were married in Southampton the day after their flight, and he now holds a government appointment in the Island of Mauritius. As to Miss Violet Hunter, she is now the head of a private school at Walsall, where I believe that she has met with considerable success.

LIBRARY OF CONGRESS

Sir Arthur Conan Doyle

1859-1930

Sir Arthur Conan Doyle was born in Edinburgh, Scotland. He was the first boy among seven children. He went to Catholic schools and then studied to be a doctor at Edinburgh University. One of his teachers there, Dr. Joseph Bell, who taught him to look at his patients' appearance very closely, was the inspiration for the great fictional detective Sherlock Holmes.

Doyle began his career as a ship's doctor, first on a whaling voyage to the Arctic when he was twenty-one and next on a steamer sailing to west Africa, where he came down with malaria. When he returned to England he opened an office in Portsmouth. A strong believer in physical fitness and very fond of sports, he played cricket and soccer for the town's teams.

To add to his income he wrote tales about medieval knights and his first Sherlock Holmes story, *A Study in Scarlet*. Thinking he would have more time for writing if he became an eye specialist, he went to Austria in 1890 to train. But he was frustrated by studying in German and returned to London, where he attracted few patients. He decided to give up his medical practice and write for his living. *The Adventures of Sherlock Holmes* came out in 1892 and brought Doyle instant fame.

It was his nature to crusade for justice and fair play. Once he used Sherlock Holmes-style techniques to get a man falsely accused of killing cattle freed from jail. He also saved another man unjustly convicted of murder.

When the Boer War broke out in South Africa in 1899, he tried to enlist as a soldier, but was too old. He was accepted as a doctor and served for no pay in a field hospital. He wrote a pamphlet explaining why the British were not guilty of cruel acts in the war. Because it softened other countries' feelings toward England, Doyle was made a knight. He strongly believed in Great Britain's Empire and her right to rule other countries. He twice ran for election to Parliament on that belief, but lost both times.

In 1911 he took part in an automobile race through Britain and Germany. He saw war coming and predicted the importance of airplanes and submarines. When World War I did break out, he said it was the climax of his life. It took the lives of his son Kingsley, his brother, and many other relatives. As the war went on, he publicly dedicated himself to spiritualism, the notion that one can talk to the dead. At great cost to his fortune and reputation, he earnestly tried to prove spiritualism is true, writing and talking about it throughout Europe and America.

Doyle wrote sixty Sherlock Holmes stories, including *The Hound of the Baskervilles*, as well as historical novels, science fiction, plays and histories of the Boer War and spiritualism. Doyle died at home of a heart attack in 1930.